TRACKS

TRACKS

DANIEL MCLINDEN

ARPress
45 Dan Road Suite 36
Canton MA 02021

Hotline: 1(888) 821-0229
Fax: 1(508) 545-7580

Ordering Information:
Quantity Sales. Special discounts are available on quantity purchases by corporations, associations, and others. For details, contact the publisher at the address above.

Printed in the United States of America.

ISBN-13   Paperback   979-8-89676-211-9
               eBook   979-8-89676-212-6

Library of Congress Control Number: 2024925150

CHAPTER 1

1900
NEW MEXICO TERRITORY

DAWN OF ANOTHER hot August day. A farmhouse, barn and adobe hut stood at the edge of a cornfield next to an oak grove. The first rays of morning light slipped through a crack in the door of the adobe hut and climbed across the sleeping face of Miguel Figueroa. Turning from the glare he buried his head under Maria's arm. The baby Pedro, lying between them, yawned, then locked his mouth onto Maria's nipple, dripping with milk.

Miguel rolled out of bed and planted his hardened soles on the dirt floor. He leaned close to Maria's ear and whispered, *"Ya me voy."* "I'm leaving now." She turned to him and covered his mouth with a warm kiss before slipping back in slumber. Miguel leaned toward the baby and nuzzled its furry head. He sat back for a moment fixed on the two of them. Maria's thick eyelashes fluttered to open. But no. Miguel grinned at her effort then left with a smile on his face.

After filling a big burlap bag with corn, Miguel set out on foot for Agua Seca, the nearest town. Making his way down the foothills his nostrils began to tingle, sensing rain. Darkening clouds began to shrink the bright morning sky ahead of him.

The rusty smell of rain took Miguel back to his first thunderstorms and rainbows over Lake Chapala near Guadalajara in the State of Jalisco, Mexico — when he was a boy.

Veins of lightning appeared and disappeared one after another giving way to crackling and rumbling sounds.

A flash flood could carry him off, he thought. He picked up pace and headed toward a large rock cluster for shelter. He climbed half way up and found cover.

Wind blew wildly. Sand swirled. The first drops of fresh rain splattered and plunked about him. More drops came, countless, crashing on the rocks and dancing on the steamy surface of the earth below. The runoff roared through washes and a hard rain lasted over an hour. Then the overcast sky broke into clouds drifting north.

The sun poked out brilliantly. To the south, deep turquoise sky stretched and faded as far as the eye could see. The sky was mirrored a thousand times in puddles dotting the landscape. Miguel stood up, took deep breaths, and slid with care from the rocks clutching the sack of corn.

—◦◦((◦))◦◦—

Agua Seca had a hotel, general store, doctor's office, telegraph office, saloon, jail, a White church, a Mexican church, a scattering of wooden houses and adobe huts. It was a little town, set in grids off the town square (*plaza*) about a day on horseback from El Paso and Juarez along the Rio Grande. A hundred or so Whites lived among the Mexicans who outnumbered them some seven to one. Nearly all the Mexican families had deep roots in the area. Whites had come and gone, mostly after the Civil War.

Miguel, from Jalisco, and Maria, from Chihuahua, were new to the area. Several months before, they first walked into town and saw a white man in a white apron, standing in front of the General Store. He was the proprietor, Duncan MacPherson. Maria's belly caught his eye so he motioned the couple over and took them inside. He poured cool water from a colorful pitcher into blue-colored glasses. Miguel and Maria thanked him, and Miguel asked him in Spanish if he knew of any work in the area. MacPherson, recognized the word for work (*trabajo*).

Miguel's facial expressions reminded MacPherson of someone. Miguel had the same look during that first meeting that MacPherson's older brother, Douglas, had had when Douglas convinced Duncan to leave England and come to America. It was a youthful look poised for adventure. Douglas had the same look after crossing the Atlantic when he convinced Duncan to join the Union Army.

Miguel was still a few years younger than Douglas was, when Douglas and Duncan fought the Rebels. Miguel was broad-shouldered, lean, tall, fit and strong, with hair, thick and black. His hands were huge and looked like they could do anything.

When MacPherson first looked into Maria's eyes they captured him. They were almond-shaped, with whites of bluish grey, rich brown irises, flecked with gold, encircled by black markings. Shiny white dots gave contrast to the glossy pupils. She had high cheekbones — *like an Indian*, MacPherson thought — thick, straight, jetblack hair. MacPherson had an eye for beauty and knew it came in all shapes and colors.

To Maria, MacPherson had kind watery eyes. The lightest blue she had ever seen. He was roughly her father's age. But, she sensed, a man not like her father. MacPherson was gentle. Not gruff. Her father could never be at ease with people, not even his six daughters, and in particular, Maria, the youngest, whose difficult birth had taken her mother from him. Maria, in coming to Agua Seca, had been miles from her father, in a new life, about to bear a child of her own for the first time. She wondered about the outcome.

She is truly a rare creature, MacPherson had thought. She was indeed. A Yaqui teenager in full bloom. MacPherson called to some Mexican youngsters playing near the store to run and find Jorge Ruiz — to have him come translate for the new arrivals.

⟫⟨●⟩⟪

Miguel owed a lot to MacPherson and looked forward to seeing him that August morning after the thunderstorm — especially, to get his response to the corn. It was after nine o'clock when Miguel let the heavy burlap sack drop gently onto wooden planks, not far from the general store, next to a water trough. He sat down for a moment on the edge of the walkway, removed his sandals and clapped them together, shooting chunks of mud in all directions. He smelled bacon frying, coming from the hotel close by. He washed his hands and face with rainwater from the trough.

Meanwhile, inside the store, MacPherson stood behind the counter looking over the books.

Miguel and his burlap sack passed through the open doorway of the store. MacPherson looked up.

"Miguel!"

"Señor MacPherson."

"How is everything?"

"Good."

"Did you get caught in the storm?"

"Dithyugethcau? *Como?* How is that?"

"*La llúvia?* The rain?"

"*Mucha.* A lot."

"You brought corn?"

"Yes. Corn."

"Well, let's see."

Miguel handed him a long green husk. MacPherson tore it open then pulled off silky golden tassels exposing bumpy white kernels. He lifted the cob to his nose and smelled its freshness. He took out a pen knife from his pocket and whittled off several rows of kernels from the cob and shared them with Miguel. "Sweet and delicious," MacPherson remarked, "I'll boil some for dinner tonight." What he would not take home he would display outside the store in big baskets with a "Penny a Piece" sign over them. The corn would not last the day.

From the wooden sidewalk came heavy sounds of clomping boots and clanking spurs.Three men entered the store. MacPherson moved away from Miguel toward them. Only the one, looking about fifty, made eye contact. He was an older version of the other two, only heavier, with a bigger head, and shorter stature. The youngest one walked passed MacPherson to Miguel and poked him in the chest. "Feels pretty lively for a cigar store Indian." His sidekicks laughed. Miguel, looking right in the eye of his taunter, did not even flinch.

MacPherson spoke. "He doesn't speak English. You're wastin' your time with him."The authority in MacPherson's voice overshadowed any politeness. MacPherson wouldn't stand for that kind of conduct.

And nothing or no one had ever frightened him. At least not since Vicksburg in July 1863 when his brother Douglas got shot dead beside him.

"Seen this fellow?" the oldest one asked, unfolding a *Wanted Poster* for MacPherson, who studied it for a moment.

"No, can't say as I have. You want to leave this for me to post in the store?"

"I only got the one. Me and my boys gonna bring him in. Don't like to share the reward."

"I'm sorry then. Can't help you."

"Okay. Give us some flour and a sack of beans. Coffee. How much for a box of ammo for a Colt .45?"

"Two bits."

"Make it a half dozen boxes."

When they left, Miguel and MacPherson did a little business of their own, going over the corn count and what things Miguel needed to take back.

"I almost forgot," MacPherson said with a faint smile coming to his lips, "I got that machete you've been asking for." MacPherson reached under the counter and produced a Mexican machete from Juarez. It was a thick-bladed knife, over two-feet long, straight on the dull side, curved on the sharp side — with a smooth wooden handle.

"*Mil gracias, Señor MacPherson.*" A thousand thanks. Miguel took the machete in hand, gripping the handle to test its comfort, and feather bouncing the whole of it to gauge the balance. He pulled the end of the handle toward his face and ran his gaze down the shaft to see how straight it was. He rotated it from side to side, beaming. Miguel put the provisions and the machete into the burlap sack.

Then he and MacPherson talked some more. Between the few words they shared, and sign language, they left it where MacPherson would come to the farm on Sunday with horse and buckboard to pick up more corn and other produce. Miguel had a quarter acre of corn planted in four sections growing a week apart; some beans, tomatoes, strawberries and melons; in terms of livestock, there were chickens, roosters, pigs and a cow; no horse. MacPherson owned the farm and supplied the feed and seed. Miguel worked it. MacPherson set aside twenty cents of every dollar he got from the farm produce for Miguel.

What corn from Sunday's trip MacPherson couldn't sell fresh would go to El Paso for milling and come back to the store, flour or meal.

MacPherson had bought the farm two years before in 1898 when he came west for health reasons, but found he was neither a farmer nor ready to retire. So he bought the General Store and let the farm go idle until Miguel and Maria showed up. MacPherson was a city product — Edinburgh, London, New York City and Washington, D.C. If his doctors hadn't told him his chronic bronchitis would kill him, he would have stayed in Georgetown, outfitting politicians from his haberdashery shop on M Street.

MacPherson had been holding onto the farm to see what his son, Andy, a medical student in Baltimore, would do, once he finished his studies and internship.

•••

Miguel got back to the farm after noon. He saw smoke coming from the tiny stove pipe sticking out of the roof of the adobe hut, and smelled beans boiling.

Maria sat on the ground in a sliver of shade in front of the hut with the baby Pedro lying beside her on a shawl napping. There was a pleasant breeze in the shade. Maria's skirt was pulled up and piled in her lap. She was slapping mud and straw on her right thigh, in layers, forming clay tiles for the roof of the hut. She had several tiles laid out in the sun to dry. Miguel came up and squatted next to her, helping her finish. He told her about the storm from his perch in the rocks and the things he had gotten from MacPherson. She filled him in on the pounding the farm had taken from the storm, the leaks in the hut, and Pedro's comical facial expressions when he heard thunder.

Miguel went to the creek and picked out a pumice stone. After dinner he would hone the machete to razor sharpness.

Late in the afternoon clouds gathered. The wind came up, carrying with it the smell of rain. It was getting dark quickly. The inside of the adobe hut was cozy, lit by a candle on a small table, and by glowing embers from the stove. Shadows danced throughout the hut.

After Maria and Miguel ate, Miguel sat at the table, sharpening the machete. Maria breastfed Pedro and put him next to the bed, in a pillowed crate, the place he started out each night but never ended up.

Maria washed the plates and spoons in a pot of hot water on the stove. Leaving the bean pot, rigged over the stove, half-full, she went outside to wash up.

It was blustery and near pitch black. *The rain is almost here*, she thought. She came inside and locked her eyes on Miguel. He looked up and seeing her expression, quietly set the machete to one side. She pulled her blouse over her head and tossed it onto the bed. She stepped out of the skirt and kicked it to where it draped over the edge of the bed, touching the floor. She grabbed the pant legs at the bottom of Miguel's trousers (*pantalones*) and whisked them off. Holding the pose at the end of the takeaway, she raised an eyebrow and mouthed the word *"Olé!"*

All the while raindrops pounded the tile roof. Miguel could hear them above his own heartbeat and Maria's quickened breathing. Then he heard the snort of a horse and muffled hoof beats. Three sets. *The bounty hunters*, he thought. Miguel had to pull out to get Maria's attention.

They threw their clothes on.

Miguel watched the cowboys walk their horses toward the front of the main house — dark, empty and locked up. It would soon be clear to the cowboys no one was there. Miguel watched them dismount and lead their horses into the barn. *The smoke from the stovepipe and the smell of the beans would bring them to the adobe hut.*

Miguel set the machete under the bed and signaled Maria to a dark corner of the room. He pushed the door open and stepped out, half way.

"Ain't that the wetback from the general store?"

"Damned if it ain't."

"You mind we spend the night in the barn?"

Miguel could only look at them. He didn't understand. They began motioning about sleeping in the barn and eating. Miguel nodded and pointed to the barn and nodded again, giving them the eating sign with his hands, pointing inside to the bean pot and nodding some more. The gestures he made got the point across.

The youngest one moved closer sniffing the beans. He looked past Miguel's shoulder tapping the door with a finger. He made out a figure in the shadowy flickering light, then the flash of Maria's eyes. His jaw slackened. The older man stepped closer. He looked past Miguel to Maria and back to Miguel. He backed off and told the boys to come with him to the barn.

The rain kept up.

Miguel brought beans and tortillas to the barn while Maria watched him through a crack in the door of the adobe hut. He disappeared into the barn.

The bounty hunters smiled, took the food, then dropped Miguel from behind with the butt of a pistol. He was out cold. They tied him up.

The old man would be first to the hut. The two boys would wait their turns in the barn and devour the grub.

Maria saw someone coming, backlit by the lantern light escaping from the barn, moving toward her in the rain. The door of the hut was ajar when he got to it. He shoved it wide open.

Maria stood between him and the bed. She began backing away slowly. He put his dripping hat on the table next to the candle, drew the gun from his holster and used it to signal her to get on the bed. She nodded nervously while unhitching her skirt and letting it fall to the floor. He pointed to her top with the gun and jerked the barrel a few times motioning her to take it off. She nodded, but held up a finger asking for time while she knelt to collect the skirt. He waited, content to look at her bare legs.

She rose slowly toward him, then turned to her right to drop the skirt on the bed. She kept turning to her right before unleashing a backhand machete blow to his arm, causing him to pull the trigger and fire an errant shot, before dropping the gun altogether. She went for his face and dealt a second blow with the sharp, thin, steel edge of the machete, splitting his right cheek and slicing open his eye.

He reached reflexively with both hands toward the wounds, too late to protect himself. The next blow, a powerful slashing forehand, severed two of his fingertips, caught in its path, and cut through the carotid artery.

He dropped to his knees. Blood poured from his wounds and spurted from his neck. He clutched at his throat. The big head made a huge target for the next strike, a two-handed chop that nearly split his skull. Maria had to pry the bloodied blade loose from his balding head.

He was left sprawled face down on the dirt floor. She picked up the pistol and stationed herself by the door. He made a series of gurgling and choking sounds — then none at all.

The two cowboys emerged from the barn, guns drawn, and walked cautiously toward the adobe hut wondering if the girl was dead from the shot that rang out.

Maria set the latch on the door and stood back, expecting them to burst through. But they took advantage of the light on the inside of the hut to peek through the crack in the door. She heard them talking and sent two bullets left and right through the door. She listened for an instant. There was only groaning. She fired another shot. No return fire. She waited a moment and opened the door. The one on the bottom looked dead. The one on top was still alive. He lifted his arm and pressed the trigger of the gun he was holding, sending a bullet into the dark and rainy night. Maria put a bullet into his face. She put another into the head of the body beneath him.

Pedro fussed slightly. Maria went to him, lifted him up and teetered with him for a moment on unsteady limbs. She laid him down, put on her skirt, looked over the three bodies for any sign of life, picked Pedro up again and went to the barn, not knowing what to expect. Miguel was just coming to.

Miguel spent the whole night covering up. He buried the men and their saddles away from the hut in a place he would keep secret from Maria. He buried their guns in a box in the barn and took the horses to a mountain meadow where he let them go before backtracking home on foot.

Maria cleaned the blood from her clothes and the earthen floor and patched the door with mud. When her breasts swelled with milk she fed Pedro.

Weeks later the Sheriff from El Paso stopped at the General Store in Agua Seca with the horses in tow and described the owners to MacPherson. MacPherson told the Sheriff that they had come through town tracking an outlaw. Likely, reckoned MacPherson and the Sheriff, the outlaw had gotten them before they got him. Later MacPherson told Miguel that the cowboy who poked him in the chest the day of the storm, along with the other two, were probably dead. Miguel only nodded.

The next summer Alicia was born. Miguel had asked MacPherson if he could add to the adobe hut now that he had two little ones but MacPherson told him to wait. If MacPherson's son stayed in the east, Miguel could move into the main house with his family.

But in August, MacPherson's son returned from medical school with a young bride. There was some question in MacPherson's mind whether the newlyweds would want Miguel, Maria and the children to stay on. But they did, glad to see the farm worked. Before the weather changed the adobe hut was doubled in size. Both Duncan and Andy helped Miguel build the addition to the hut.

Andy and Sheila planned to travel together by buckboard to Agua Seca where he would assist Doc Stone and make house calls while she would teach school. Andy had just graduated from Johns Hopkins; Sheila from Oberlin College in Ohio. She was the daughter of a Philadelphia lawyer who loved to bet on the ponies. Andy and Sheila had met in Baltimore at the Pimlico Race Track three years before, at the running of the Preakness.

Sheila was thin and pale, with green eyes and strawberry blonde hair. Her eastern clothes hung beautifully on her. She thought she could grow to love the West. She was certain not one ounce of her would miss the rigid conventions of Main Line society. When her own children came she would stop teaching. Andy, for his part, was mad about Sheila, glad to be near his dad, and willing to sacrifice the pace and excitement of a big city hospital for a practice of his own someday.

Over the years the Figueroa family grew. And every year Sheila prayed she'd get pregnant. But it didn't happen.

When Pedro was five, Sheila taught him to read.

When old Doc Stone died, Andy's duties doubled. He had learned a great deal from Doc Stone, a battlefield medic turned family practitioner. One thing Andy did a lot more than Doc Stone had done, was care for the Mexicans. Often Andy would take Miguel with him on house calls to translate.

When Pedro was ten, Mexico erupted in revolution and all the border towns, including Agua Seca, started to swell with the fleeing population. More and more Andy treated the sick and wounded who came to town.

One morning Ricardo Sanchez made his way beyond Agua Seca across a patch of desert into the foothills toward the smell of smoke mixed with boiling beans. He came to a bend in a road a few hundred yards from the MacPherson farm and collapsed.

Dogs found him first and surrounded him, barking and howling. Pedro and the other children ran down the road to the dogs then back to Maria with news of a man lying on the ground, barely breathing.

Maria made a litter, and with the help of the children, dragged Ricardo to the barn. He came to, still dazed, drank water, and passed out again. He smelled of vomit, urine and feces. He seemed at death's door. Maria stayed with him, washed his face and hands and gave him water when he woke and tried to feed him tortilla soup. At one point he grabbed her and struggled with her, apparently hallucinating, before weakening and letting go.

When Andy came home he examined the man. He had typhoid fever. Andy told everyone to stay clear of the patient. Andy stripped him of his clothes and had Miguel burn them. Then Andy had Miguel boil water. Andy hand-bathed Ricardo. He directed Miguel to put the big basin behind the adobe hut, and fill it with boiling water so Maria, when it cooled down just enough, could bathe in it. "Burn her clothes and have her change into fresh ones."

Andy had the children come into the main house to sleep. After a few days Andy would know if Ricardo would survive and if Maria had been infected. At next light Andy planned to set out for Agua Seca with Miguel, ask after Ricardo, put folks on the lookout for symptoms, post warnings, and look for any more cases.

As Maria bathed in the big basin, Sheila collected clean clothes to give to her. Sheila took the lantern from the dining table in the main house for the short walk to the back of the adobe hut. Maria stood up. Steamy vapors from the hot water floated from her body. She reached for the clothes. *In this light Carravaggio would be layering his canvas with her*, Sheila thought.

Ricardo died in two days. Maria and Miguel took ill.

Pedro sat on a chair in the adobe hut beside the bed of his parents listening to his father tell him of the great walk he had taken from Guadalajara, meeting his mother along the way, and, the night of the bounty hunters. Pedro was eleven. He looked deep into his mother's loving eyes and wondered how she could have fended off three men.

Miguel and Maria were buried under a White Oak tree near the creek. Andy had Pedro help him make two wooden crosses. Together they painted the crosses white. Alicia, Martin, Eduardo and Ana were ten, nine, seven, and five. There was no question Sheila and Andy would raise the children. Duncan MacPherson suggested that Andy start taking Pedro on rounds with him like he had done with Miguel.

After the dinner that no one ate on the evening of the burial, Pedro sat in the parlor with Sheila, Doctor Andy and Duncan. Pedro listened to them with a single thought in the back of his mind, *his parents were gone.* Nothing could bring them back, and if only that man had not stumbled into their lives.

That night Pedro could not sleep. He did not want to visit the sick with Doctor Andy. If anything, he wanted to run the farm. But German Rodriguez was coming for that. Pedro did not like German Rodriguez because he sensed his mother had not liked him either, the few times he had come to the farm. Pedro decided that he had to leave. *To escape,* he thought. *He could not stay on without his parents. Doctor Andy and Sheila would take good care of his brothers and sisters. Some day he would come back. But he had to go.*

He left a note saying he was going to El Paso to find work. He was sorry but he could not live on the farm without his parents. He went north instead. Andy would have tracked him down in no time if Pedro had told the truth. Pedro carried a burlap sack with a bed roll, some food, a canteen, his father's machete, and a box, with three Colt .45s in it, dug up from the barn floor.

All in all he had a heavy load for a little boy.

CHAPTER II

1911

PEDRO LOOKED DOWN on a gilded valley. A small farmhouse, with smoke spiraling from a stovepipe, sat below the eastern side of a ridge. The sun was going down. A creek ran along the western slope flanked by grass and trees. A lone figure was walking from the creek, carrying a basket. As Pedro got closer to the farmhouse he could see it was a young girl whose pace quickened when she saw him.

She disappeared into the farmhouse and from it a man came out to meet him. In broken Spanish he asked Pedro, "*Dondyvaz*? (Where ya headed)?"

"I'm going to Albuquerque."

"You have family there?"

"No."

"Where's your family."

"I don't have any."

"You an orphan?"

It was the first time anyone had asked the question. It was hard to answer.

"*Sí.*"

"Wash up over there and come in. It's dinner time."

The inside was much starker than Sheila and Andy's. Smaller too. The woman was Mexican. A little lighter than Pedro. The man was White. The boy looked at Pedro curiously. He must have been Eduardo's age, and dark like the woman. The girl would only look at

Pedro when he was not looking at her. Her features were sharp like the man's. Her coloring, a blend of the man and the woman. Green eyes, with black lashes and brows, rosy lips, and dark brown hair. Flaring nostrils. Pedro could see the shape of breasts under her blouse. She was fourteen. Three years older than Pedro.

The man asked him if he knew anything about farming. When he said he did, the man asked him to stay on to do some haying and other chores. When the man searched for his next word in broken Spanish, Pedro filled in the pause with the correct word in English. They began conversing in English. The children followed along but the woman strained. After dinner, the woman argued with the man about letting Pedro stay. Another mouth to feed. But the man had the last word. Pedro would sleep in the barn and carry his weight, or go packing.

Pedro stayed busy. He liked the man, Señor Mike O'Donnell. The woman had nothing but contempt for Pedro and told her children he was dirty and to stay away from him. Pedro had little contact with them, except meals, under the woman's icy gaze.

Pedro became Mike's right arm and after the corn harvest Pedro was supposed to go with him to town. Knowing how excited Pedro was to be going to town, the woman insisted he stay behind and clean the chicken coop instead. It was the worst job on the place. Señor O'Donnell gave in to her.

Pedro cleaned the coop in no time. Without telling her he was done, and stinking to high heaven, he went off to the creek. The girl, Genoveva, was there washing clothes. She stood waist deep in slowly moving water next to a big rock, slapping and rubbing the few clothes, her family members were not wearing, against it.

The mid-morning sun shone through the trees.

Pedro stopped in his tracks when he saw Genoveva's dappled figure from behind. The thick dark hair, goldenly lit at the top, cascaded into black wet strands clinging to the nape of her neck. She was humming. Pedro walked a little ways down the bank to get closer.

"Genoveva."

She turned quickly to the sound of her name. "You scared me."

"I'm sorry."

"What are you doing here. Didn't Mama have you cleaning the chicken coop?"

"I finished."

Genoveva looked surprised. "That was quick. Did you do a good job?"

"Yes. But I don't know if she'll like it."

"Didn't you show it to her?"

"No. It was so hot and I smell so bad I had to come down here."

"You're probably going to get into trouble."

"I know."

"Did you know I was here?"

"No."

"Oh."

They both pondered the question and answer. Genoveva held up a bar of soap, "Might as well just throw me your clothes."

Pedro thought for a second. It was not what he wanted to do. She was looking at him with a gleeful smile. She liked to embarrass him. Like the time she nudged him and pointed to her father's horse when it sported a hardon. "I'll just go in clothes and all."

"Suit yourself."

He waded in. "What happened to your parents."

"They died of typhoid fever."

"What's that?"

"A disease. It comes from dirty conditions. War. Revolution."

"What's that?"

"They are fighting in Mexico against a dictator, Porfirio Diaz."

"How do you know these things?"

"I lived on a farm with my parents and..."

She interrupted,"Were they Mexican or White or both like mine?"

"Mexican. But we lived on a White man's farm. He is a doctor and his wife is a school teacher. I learned English from them and she taught me to read."

"You can read?"

"Yes."

"I can't. I want to learn."

"What about your father. Why doesn't he teach you?"

"He can't read."

"Your mother?"

"No."

A distant call shattered the conversation,"Genoveva! Genoveva!"

"Hide!"

Pedro slipped across the creek behind some rocks on the other side.

"Genoveva, have you seen that boy?"

"No, Mama. Maybe he went to the fields."

"Aren't you done?"

"Yes, Mama. I just finished."

"Well come on."

Pedro watched Genoveva get out and collect the clothes with her mother.

"Take your wet clothes off, Genoveva. Change into these." Her mother had a skirt and blouse for her.

"I'll change in the house," she said.

She allowed her mother to get ahead of her before turning around and looking back at Pedro. She smiled slightly. Pedro smiled back.

———◦《◦》◦———

Señor O'Donnell came back with news of Statehood and a big ball in Albuquerque to celebrate it. Genoveva asked him if he could get some books next time he went to town. She told him she wanted to learn to read. *The nearest school was too far*, he reasoned, *How could she expect to teach herself?*

"Pedro can read."

"How do you know?"

"I asked him."

"It figgers. He's smart as a whip. Speaks two languages perfeck."

Next time Señor O'Donnell went to Albuquerque he came back with a copy of "Huckleberry Finn" from the town library.

That night Pedro was flanked at the table by Genoveva and her brother. Pedro pointed to word after word pronouncing each one making his way down the page. Then he started at the top again and went word by word, one sentence at a time. He handed the book to Genoveva to have her repeat the words and the sentence. It was not easy. Her brother tried too. They both learned a couple of words that first evening. The mother seethed at allowing the young vagabond to take over the family.

Over the next few weeks the children stayed on the first pages of the book. Pedro had them learn the alphabet at the same time and try to write words from the sounds of the alphabet that they were learning.

He gave them the same exercises Sheila had given him. Before long they were reading. Then everyone started to listen carefully to the words of Mark Twain and what it was like to be a young boy on the Mississippi. They were curious listeners, frequently interrupting to ask what words meant. Señor O'Donnell had to explain slavery to the three youngsters.

Pedro had a soothing voice. When he read, Genoveva leaned toward the pages of the book, often with her head blocking Pedro's line of sight. He put up with it, gladly, to smell her hair and relish in her scent. He crooked his neck to see around her. The first time her breast brushed against his arm it excited him. Genoveva liked the altered state she felt nudging her breast against Pedro's arm, listening to him read. It was an elixir for the two of them.

⎯⎯⎯⎯ ◦((◦))◦ ⎯⎯⎯⎯

Eldon Johnson owned the feed store in Albuquerque. "Mike, my wife is making dresses for the ladies goin' to the Statehood Ball. You and the missus 're goin,' aren't ya?"

"Hadn't really thought about it."

"Well, it's only gonna happen once. You don't wanna miss it. There'll be a parade. You and I can put on are old Army uniforms. What da ya say?"

"Can your wife let them out?"

After Eldon's chuckle, Mike added, "I'll talk to Graciela."

Graciela O'Donnell wanted nothing to do with socializing. She had little English or any desire for hefty white women looking down on her and talking about her, the way they did when she went to town. But she had an idea. She told Mike to get a dress for Genoveva and take her instead. It was about time she met some boys. Old enough to start a family. The Mexicans marked a girl's womanhood at fifteen with a *quinceanera* (fifteenth year) celebration. Genoveva would not get one. So let her go to the Statehood Ball.

⎯⎯⎯⎯ ◦((◦))◦ ⎯⎯⎯⎯

Albuquerque teemed with people from all over. When Mike and Genoveva arrived, the town was abuzz with news of a runaway buckboard whose team had trampled two boys trying to get across the main street.

One boy was dead and the other in a coma. Gunshots were fired by drunken statehooders every few minutes and the place was a circus. Mike took Genoveva to the Cathedral. He always took the family there whenever he brought them to town. It was a big, beautiful building, cool and quiet inside, with the fragrance of incense. Genoveva said a prayer for the boys.

When the Civil War vets paraded, a band played "The Battle Hymn of the Republic." Duncan MacPherson was there, marching. So were Andy and Sheila, watching. After the parade, MacPherson commented to Andy and Sheila, "Instead of a Union victory, we should be honoring the dead on both sides."

"But you fought for the North and Uncle Douglas was killed by a Rebel."

"Yes, I did," MacPherson paused, "and Douglas was. Lincoln should have let the slaves come north to freedom and let the South secede. Southerners would have been begging to come back into the Union and begging for a labor force, even if they had to pay for it, and a lot of good men from both sides would still be here."

"Pop, I think you are the only man alive to espouse that theory." "You might be right, Andy. But that's the point. Try taking a poll of the dead and see if the majority don't go along with me. But their votes'll never count, now will they?"

"I think you're right, Duncan" said Sheila, squeezing his arm as they strolled together.

"Well, if my time came to serve, I'd go," Andy objected.

"Make damn sure it's worth the price, son. See if the politicians, and the people who own them, have a cause, better than greed, to fight for. I suppose I wouldn't stand in your way, regardless, you being a doctor. You can go piece together and sew up all the young idealists, the sadists, the criminally insane, and the vast majority of dupes and pawns, like I was, who do their government's bidding."

With good-natured sarcasm, Andy replied, "You make it sound so patriotic, Pop."

"Well son, in the beginning it is patriotic. In the end it's a mistake."

"Let's go get ready for the Ball," Sheila said, saddened by the political talk.

Genoveva wore a frilly lavender dress to the Ball. The women watching her saw prime competition for their daughters. The men, of all ages, could not keep their eyes off her. It was the exotic mixture. Almost a grown woman. Rich teenage palette. When Sheila first caught sight of Genoveva, Sheila's memory flickered for an instant on Maria.

Eldon Johnson's son, Garth, wore a dark grey woolen pin-striped suit, his mother had made for him. He had uncontrollable hair, darkened to a ruddy brown from gobs of pink pomade. He and Judge Watson's son, James, had gotten drunk together during the day's festivities. James got sick and went home. Garth sat in a stupor in the corner of the ballroom. He could not keep his eyes off the girl in the lavender dress. His mother found him and poured coffee down him for the rest of the evening. He refused to go home. His father's own drinking left him oblivious to what was going on with the son. The mother had her hands full, between the two men in her life. *Devil liquor*, she thought. The only saving grace for her was seeing her handiwork swaying on display across the dance floor.

Genoveva spoke briefly with Mrs. Johnson, thanking her for the beautiful dress. Mrs. Johnson thought for a moment about introducing Genoveva to Garth but his condition prevented it. Drink was ruining the night.

In the end no one had the nerve to approach Genoveva. She had stood close to her father the whole evening and the look on his face did not appear to be an invitation to dance with his daughter. He was not as keen as Graciela to get her started with boys.

The next day Genoveva told Pedro all about Albuquerque, the festivities and the tragedy surrounding the two boys who got run over. Pedro wanted to tell her how nice she had looked in the dress but could not get the words out.

Eldon Johnson had his son Garth deliver feed to the O'Donnell farm. Pedro saw him coming. Tall, when he stepped from the buckboard, with sandy hair.

"Is Mr. O'Donnell here?"

"I'll get him," Pedro replied.

Mike O'Donnell was in the barn making a chair. His son was watching him do it.

"Señor O'Donnell there is someone here." Mike O'Donnell had put down his saw the moment he first heard the buckboard approach and was walking out of the barn when Pedro made the superfluous announcement.

"Hello Garth."

"Mr. O'Donnell."

"Your dad told me he wanted you to learn the business, meet customers, see their farms."

"Yes, Sir."

"Fine."

Señor O'Donnell introduced the boys to Garth. No handshakes. Señor O'Donnell and Garth stuck their heads into the house and said hello to Graciela and Genoveva. Genoveva's hair was up and wild. She was leaning forward on a rolling pin, flattening dough on the kitchen table. She had flour on her forehead.

Señor O'Donnell and Garth walked the place. Graciela had some sweet rolls and lemonade ready for them when they got back. All the way home Garth tried to figure a way to get back to the O'Donnell place. *Maybe on a Sunday. Stop by and say I was on my way home from hunting.*

Over the next several months Garth made a half-dozen visits.

He never told his parents anything about Genoveva.

Pedro and Genoveva would meet secretly whenever they could and talk about their dreams. Not nighttime ones, but what life had in store for them. Reading had bound them close together and loosened their imaginations. *Huckleberry Finn, Tom Sawyer, The Gift of the Magi,* a number of pulp westerns, even newspapers, all from the library in Albuquerque.

After one of Garth's Sunday visits, Genoveva asked Pedro what he thought of him. "I don't know anything about him or why he keeps coming here," Pedro said. She did not press the issue, sensing that Garth was the last person Pedro wanted to bring into their world, and shatter it. Garth was a man, almost, she thought, Pedro, still a boy, and she was not a little girl anymore.

⸺⸺⟪◉⟫⸺⸺

Garth came out one Sunday in a suit, the same one he had worn to the Statehood Ball, bringing flowers and chocolate to Genoveva. He held out a ring. The whole thing caught her off guard. She said she would think about it. He asked if he could come the following Sunday for her answer.

Her mother was for it. Her father was surprised by the proposal. The choice was simple for Graciela. She did not believe in fairytale romances or perfect marriages. *Mike was a good man*, she thought, *and Garth might become one.* Still Garth would have something Mike never had. Money. She insisted Genoveva marry Garth.

Genoveva lay in her favorite spot — with her hands folded behind her head — beside the creek with the spring sun bearing down on her. She saw red, orange and magenta images when she closed her eyes. Garth was coming in two hours. She listened to the birds, the insects, the running creek, and wind rustling in the trees. Her face grew warmer and she felt like she could melt. Her mother's words about the marriage bed were ringing in her ears.

A shadow came over her. It was Pedro. "What should I do? Should I marry him?"

"Your decision."

She hated the answer. She wanted him to say *No.* She looked into his eyes. They were saying *No.* She wished he was old enough to take her away. But then she was distracted. Her forehead crinkled. He felt her staring at the new black hairs on his upper lip and saw her face twist into a curious expression. She stroked the burgeoning mustache with her index finger and smiled coyly. He braced for what she might say. He sensed the cogs in the wheels of her brain winding up. He knew how mischievous she got. Her remarks could be funny and cutting.

"Come over here," she said, getting up and walking closer to the creek.

She looked to the farmhouse and saw no one. "Kiss me." She put her arms around his neck.

The statement was neither funny nor cutting; rather, serious. Pedro watched as she closed her eyes and waited for the kiss. He pecked softly at her lips.

She kissed him back. The kiss went on.

What was she doing? she asked herself. She felt sensations more intense than the dreamy ones she had at night or the ones she got from leaning into Pedro as he read to her. The two of them were pressed together.

She pushed him away and looked down at his pants. Just like the horse.

She looked toward the farmhouse. No sign of life.

She looked into Pedro's eyes. She and Pedro were just kids but the exchange was timeless.

She took his hand and put it under her blouse.

She looked toward the farmhouse and saw no one. Everyone else was busy inside getting ready for Garth.

"Lie down," she said. He lay on his back.

She brushed over him with her torso.

She pushed his pants down and pulled up her skirt.

The breathing got heavier and a connection was made. There was no turning back.

She let out huge sighs as her heart skipped beats. She could hear his heart thumping out loud.

Pedro could not hold back. Neither could she.

"*Te quiero, Genoveva.*"

"I love you, Genoveva" he said when they stopped.

"I love you, Pedro, and always will."

She looked over at the farmhouse. Still quiet.

She composed herself, lying still on top of him for a moment, except for mild aftershocks.

Dripping perspiration onto his face, already doused in its own, she insisted he not move. The bright sun behind her gave her a golden crown. When her mouth angled again for his, the sun came out from behind her head and blinded him.

They did it again.

Still no sign of life from the farmhouse.

Genoveva married Garth and had Pedro's baby. Pedro had left the farm the day after she told him she would marry Garth. So Pedro was already gone before any sign of a baby. The timing of the birth pointed to Pedro as the father. The baby's face sealed it for Genoveva.

Garth and his family had difficulty with the child's darkness. He looked a lot like his grandmother, Graciela, to them. Nothing like a Johnson.

Genoveva learned to sew and prospered along with her in-laws. She liked sex but did not have the passion for Garth that she had had for Pedro. Garth would climb onto her late at night, drunk, coming back from card games in the saloon. His whisky breath was bad. Tobacco made it worse.

She often thought of Pedro by the creek.

CHAPTER III

1916

WAR CAME AFTER the sinking of the Lusitania. America was finally in. The New Mexico regiment went to France. It was not until the end of the campaign that Garth and Andy MacPherson met in a field hospital.

Looking for things in common they exchanged distinct recollections of the Statehood Ball years before in Albuquerque. When Garth told Andy he had married the girl in the lavender dress, Andy said, he knew just who he meant.

Garth, a sniper, had been brought in, mildly blinded by mustard gas, but worse, severely depressed with combat fatigue. Andy MacPherson, commissioned a lieutenant, had been doctoring and triaging near the Maginot Line, also to the point of exhaustion. The noise and the quiet were getting to them. There was no rest.

Garth gradually got his sight back. But his depression did not end. In another week he'd go back to the front.

Doctor MacPherson was taking a bullet out of a soldier, and a nurse was changing Garth's dressings, when an errant bomb tore through the painted cross on the side of the large tent they occupied with dozens of others. Andy MacPherson was burned beyond recognition and Garth and the nurse took shrapnel. The three of them were among the many dead.

The Germans apologized for what they called a regrettable accident of war. Duncan MacPherson called it senseless.

Both Andy MacPherson and Garth Johnson received praise for having served their country in what came to be called "The Great War" and "The War To End All Wars" in separate funerals in Agua Seca and Albuquerque, a few weeks apart. Sheila and Genoveva each returned home from their respective services for their fallen husbands with an American Flag — neatly folded.

Duncan MacPherson, at 78, had been living for Andy's safe return and for the end of the war. He saw neither. He died on November 3, 1918.

⸺ ◉ ⸺

That same year Pedro arrived in Socorro, New Mexico, after having worked on a farm near Santa Fe since leaving the O'Donnells. The local Sheriff in Socorro, seeing him loitering about town, offered him two bits to bury a stray dog, then got him work on the Hollister sheep ranch about a half mile out of town.

Over the next two years Pedro was paired with another teenager named Antonio Flores. They tended the sheep, taught the dogs tricks, and became expert marksmen with a .22 rifle. Pedro taught Antonio, an avid learner with the keenest of minds, English and how to read and write it from newspapers Mr. Hollister would discard. During the long nights, Pedro thought of his parents, his siblings, the MacPhersons, and the O'Donnells. Genoveva always haunted him, particularly when Antonio strummed an old guitar and sang sad love songs. Antonio tried to teach Pedro to play, but it was no use.

⸺ ◉ ⸺

A theatrical troupe was coming to Socorro. The billing featured, "The Incomparable Stage Actor, Liam Sullivan," and "The Golden Voice of Mary Florentine," with Broadway tunes and dancers. It cost one dollar to get in. Pedro and Antonio went to town on a Saturday night for the first time ever. They stood in line in front of the saloon to buy tickets, but were turned away. No Mexicans. Pedro was disappointed but not surprised. Antonio pressed on, *"Vamos Pedro, alla atras."* "Come on, Pedro, let's go around back."

They found a way in and made their way up a back staircase. They followed it to a balcony and, seeing some beams overhead, hoisted themselves up and nested there, in the very back, high above everyone else, for a bird's eye view of the performance.

Liam Sullivan told some funny stories about traveling around the country, and talked about politicians, getting more laughs. Then he signaled for the lights to dim. Pedro and Antonio noticed a young man taking to the beam across from them to operate a spotlight.

The darkened saloon with the lone spotlight on Liam Sullivan invited quiet. You could hear a pin drop. In a soft whisper he began with, "That you have wronged me doth appear in this. You have condemned and noted Lucius Pella for taking bribes here of the Sardians wherein my letters praying on his side because I knew the man were slighted off." Moving directly opposite from where he had stood, he changed his voice, as if a different person, and said, "You wronged yourself to write in such a case. In such a time as this it is not mete that every nice offence should bear his comment." This back and forth went on for some time. Not only was he playing two characters, it seemed as if he could have been speaking Greek so far as most people in the saloon could tell. But gradually a few recognizable words came out and it had something to do with the likes of Cassius, Brutus, Caesar, and at its most dramatic with "Friends, Romans and countrymen."

To Pedro's surprise the saloon did not remain quiet and by the time Mr. Sullivan was done you could hear a few glasses clinking, whispers here and there, and one man trying to stifle a laugh.

Mary Florentine had the voice of an angel. She was lovely. After her, two young men and two young ladies, not much older than Pedro and Antonio, came out and tap danced and waltzed to several tunes coming from a wind-up Victrola. When the dancers were done Mr. Sullivan announced an intermission and invited everyone to keep drinking. Beer and whisky had been flowing the whole time.

When Mr. Sullivan returned to the stage he started in again, but this time playing a single character.

"Hey you!" a man pointing at Pedro and Antonio, yelled, "get down from there."

The interruption caught everyone off guard. "What is it?" Sullivan asked.

"Them damn Mexicans snuck in and are hanging from the rafters," the man reported. Everyone in the place looked up to where the man was pointing. To make matters worse, the spotlight left Sullivan and landed on Pedro and Antonio.

Sullivan said, "Calm down folks," and the spotlight returned to him. "Let them be. Now let's get on with the show."

"The hell you will," yelled a big burly drunk, "those stinkin' Mexicans are outta here."

"Excuse me, Sir. Let's not mar the evening for everyone. They aren't bothering anybody. They have as much right to be in here as you do."

"As I do?"

"Yes."

"To hell with you, Hamlet. I want my money back!"

The crowd was getting unruly. The owner of the saloon was making his way toward Sullivan.

"What is it folks?" Sullivan pleaded. "How will it be. You want the Mexicans out?"

Their unified response hit Sullivan unexpectedly. A resounding "Yeah!"

"Max," Mr. Sullivan said signaling, "get up here and bring the strong box."

A little man in a crumpled brown suit limped his way on stage with a steel box in his hands. Mr. Sullivan's great baritone voice announced, "Max here will be at the door so each of you, wants to, can get your money back on the way out."

The crowd was shocked. A chorus of boos rang out. Several projectiles flew near Sullivan. He stood his ground. The saloon owner was pleading with him to throw the Mexicans out and get on with it.

Sullivan wouldn't yield.

Two thirds of the patrons filed out. Some stayed on to keep drinking. The rest drew closer to the stage. Mr. Sullivan invited Pedro and Antonio down to sit at a table and said, "Bartender, bring them a couple beers and put it on my tab."

The owner said, "No." He was getting increasingly livid with Sullivan for running things. He looked at Sullivan and scowled, "No. The show is over. That's it."

Sullivan motioned to Mary to come over. He sent her after the Mexicans. She led them out of the saloon and walked them to the edge of town, where, before long the performers gathered.

Sullivan wanted to say something before he went back to his hotel. "May I say something?" He told the boys that his own people, the Sullivans on his father's side and the McConvilles on his mother's side, had come from Ireland and no one wanted them in this country. "It might have been because they were starving, uneducated and diseased when they got here," he quipped, "but they worked hard, went to school, and obeyed the laws," he paused for just the right amount of time, "except for Uncle Frank. He became a cop and was always on the take." Everyone laughed."You boys got to do the same thing as my folks did. Work hard. Raise a family. Make sure your kids get to school. Your day will come. This is a great country. Look, we got rid of slavery. Things get better all the time. Lives are lived in stages. Look at the caterpillar, crawling about, making little tracks on the ground, and then it's into a cocoon, and before long, it's flying about, a butterfly."

It occurred to Pedro that Sullivan had lost money that night over a couple of Mexicans and had stood up to a raucous crowd. He was the first person Pedro recalled to put Pedro on the same level as a White.

⸺⸺◉⸺⸺

A few months later, Antonio asked Pedro to go with him to Los Angeles where he had a cousin. Pedro thought about it, but did not want to put any more distance between himself and his family. Pedro was not ready to go back to Agua Seca but if he went all the way to Los Angeles, he could not imagine ever coming back to New Mexico. Antonio said he would write Pedro care of Hollister Ranch and let him know how he was getting on.

⸺⸺◉⸺⸺

Antonio got a job as a water boy with the Red Car Line on a new stretch of track being laid on Melrose Avenue west of Vermont Avenue. He lived with his cousin, the cousin's wife and their five children in a two-room bungalow in Boyle Heights in East Los Angeles. He slept on a bed roll in the living room. He had to get up at five-thirty in the morning and was lucky to make it home by seven at night. He missed the hills of New Mexico, the vast starry nights, Pedro, the dogs — more than the sheep — but not the cold or the heat.

Antonio's foreman, big, powerful, Hans Steuben, pushed himself and his crews hard. He couldn't help it. He had spent several years on the Big Dig in Panama and wouldn't let anyone forget it. He was tough as nails. Unlike many of the men, Antonio didn't mind Hans at all. Antonio was smart enough to stay ahead in his work. And Hans liked that. Soon Hans had Antonio doing other jobs.

⸺ ⧁ ⸺

It was the first letter Pedro ever got. Antonio went on about Los Angeles and his work on the railway. Pedro was still not about to head for California, but he had heard of good paying jobs on the Union Pacific. So he left Socorro for Grand Junction, Colorado. He met a girl there who lived two doors down from him in the same shanty town with her sister, the sister's husband and three children. The girl took care of the children. She was seventeen. Pedro was twenty. She was sweet and hardworking and told him that her sister wanted her to leave and have a family of her own. Pedro had waited too long to write to Andy and Sheila. He'd probably never go back now. Genoveva. Well. She was his first love. But married. Pedro had no idea that Garth and Doctor Andy had died in the war.

Pedro married Teresa and worked on the railroad. They began having children of their own. They named their first child, a boy, Leo. Every year another child came.

Pedro and his family eventually ended up in Smithton, Utah, a repair station for the Union Pacific. There was a foundry in nearby Spanish Fork that hired migrant Mexican workers, and a sulfur mine not far away, near Santaquin, the next town down the track, that also hired migrants.

On the east end of Smithton, in a gully, a cluster of small houses, shacks really, housed most of the Mexicans. About twenty-five families in all.

Smithton, Spanish Fork and Santaquin were each about seven miles apart in the western shadow of the Wasatch Mountains some sixty miles south of Salt Lake City, where years before, Brigham Young and his followers, the Mormons, heading west, had come through a gap in the mountains, looked down on a rich valley below, and proclaimed, "This is the place."

After two years Hans Steuben made Antonio a railman. He was in charge of six gangs. Antonio's best workers were two brothers, Hovanes and Ara Avakian. They lived in Montebello and had an even longer commute to work than Antonio.

CHAPTER IV

1925

PEDRO TOOK LEO to his first day of school. Leo was the first Mexican to attend school in Smithton. Pedro talked a couple other families into sending their children too. There was Eddy Velasco and Beatriz Ordonez. Leo, Eddy and Beatriz were classmates for years. The Mexicans celebrated Cinco de Mayo (5th of May) each year at a spot near the foot of the Wasatch Mountains in a meadow by a runoff. They called it Arroyo Bello. The Indians had called it Rawitna. The fun started with a baseball game, then barbecue, then music and dancing. Both Leo and Eddy had played in the baseball games from early on, backing up the men and shagging foul balls like two little speed demons. Beer drinking spanned all events but the Mormons only allowed a watered down version sold in the state.

⊰⊹⊱

In 1927, a good year for newspaper sales with the world heaping praise on Lucky Lindy, and America counting off each of Babe Ruth's home runs, Hans Steuben hired a bull of a man named Alex Turkmenen. He could do the work of three men. Antonio found it a bit odd that the Avakian brothers stayed clear of Turkmenen, going out of their way to avoid him, since they were all from the same part of the world.

Antonio had a plan to get them together and increase work production. He asked the Avakians to form a gang with Turkmenen because Antonio believed that Turkmenen and the Avakians together could keep pace with any of the other four-man gangs. He thought they could be the model of efficiency. The Avakians refused. Antonio offered to raise their pay but the Avakians still refused to work with Turkmenen.

<hr>

Turkmenen and his crew were laying asphalt and putting down track. A truck hauling asphalt to them rambled too close to an iron lamppost, standing exposed on a dug up sidewalk, and knocked against it. It did not seem like much of a crash but the lamppost gave way toppling onto Turkmenen as he turned to the sound of the truck hitting it.

The lamppost caught Turkmenen full force, knocking him to the ground where he quivered beneath it. The Avakians rushed over. Antonio ran after them to see them standing over Turkmenen whose chest must have been crushed. "Help me," Turkmenen was whispering, blood trickling from the side of his mouth. The Avakians initially only looked at him and shook their heads *No*. Then they looked quickly at each other. Each Avakian had rippling muscles and a perfect build. Their light skin was covered in dark hair, except for the very tops of their shiny bald heads. "Damn it" they cursed in unison, squatting and lifting the heavy iron lamppost off the downed Turkmenen.

Turkmenen died anyway, on the way to the hospital. But before the ambulance came he used up his last words on the Avakians. "Very sorry," he whispered. Antonio heard the apology and wondered what it was for.

Antonio asked the Avakians why they had hesitated in helping Turkmenen.

"Becose we Armenian," Ara said. That was the extent of the explanation.

Antonio asked Steuben if he knew what being Armenian had to do with the Avakians disliking Turkmenen. Steuben told Antonio about the Turks killing over a million Armenians in 1915, taking whole villages on death marches ending in starvation, but only after the Turks had raped, tortured, bludgeoned, stabbed and killed countless others.

Turkmenen had confessed to Steuben that he had been a Turkish soldier and hated himself for it. The Avakians, so far as Steuben knew, did not know Turkmenen had been involved in the massacre, but the hatred was so deeply felt that no Armenian would lift a hand for a Turk, not even a dying one.

Except decent ones like the Avakians, Antonio thought. Antonio admired the Avakians. In the weeks to come Antonio made an effort to find out more about Armenia and the massacre. He talked to some Armenians in Boyle Heights and read a library book on Armenian history.

He learned a new word, genocide, and analogized the Armenians to the American Indian. History he had read showed him an endless succession of invaders coming and killing off peoples, *including Mexicans*, it finally occurred to him, and the taking of land. *The discovery of gold in California*, he noted, *prompted the United States into the only pre-emptive war in its history and the discovery pushed the Mexican border from the Oregon-Alta California border hundreds of miles south. In some ways,* it also occurred to him, *it was a repeat of the whole Aztec Empire succumbing to Spain's search for gold.*

There was a sizeable community of displaced Armenians in Los Angeles and Antonio's acquaintance with it was growing. He became more friendly with the Avakians and asked them about Armenia.

They told him a few things, mainly generalities, keeping personal events to themselves.

In butchered English, Antonio received an invitation from Ara Avakian. "You coming Sunday Santa Monica beach for picnic, OK?"

Antonio, surprised, nodded, "What time?"

"One o'clock."

⚬

It took Antonio a couple hours to get to the beach in Santa Monica. He took his usual bus downtown to First and Broadway. He bought two freshly killed chickens from an outdoor Sunday market. He cut over to Wilshire Boulevard to catch the Red Line to Santa Monica.

It was a hot, sunny day, good for the beach. He rented a bathing suit and a locker when he got there.

He felt out of place with the Avakians and several other families from Montebello, with their strange language and undivided attention to smoldering wood pits. They had no interest in the surf. None of the Armenians had even rented a bathing suit.

Ara took the chickens from Antonio and set them on a board near the wood pit. "I give you chicken to my sister, Annee. She going prepare it. I going cook it."

"Thanks." Antonio looked around for the sister but she never materialized. She had gone for a walk with two other girls.

There was a block of ice and a couple of buckets. They chopped the ice and buried several containers of beer and Coca Cola in it.

"You want going swimming, go ahead," Ara said to Antonio.

"OK, I'm going in."

Antonio walked to the edge of the water. It had a unique smell, intensely fresh. The warm sand felt good under his bare feet. He took a few steps into the water. Cool bubbly foam rolled over his toes and up to his ankles and rolled away. A mild breeze filled with ocean spray christened him time and again. Standing for a moment in wet sand he sank into his own footprints.

The rhythmic crash of waves never let up; voices of children playing, and the cawing of seagulls, all mixed with the sound of the surf. He walked further into the ocean, slowly. The water was cold. He jumped over some little waves then into a big one. It was invigorating. He could taste the salt water in his mouth and through his nose. He played in the waves, catching several of them that hurled him toward shore.

He came out refreshed and stood at the water's edge to dry off in the sun and breeze. He looked out at sea, then north, and south toward the pier. Then he turned to look at the cliffs on the other side of the highway along the coast. He thought about the day the Avakians lifted the lamppost off Turkmenen.

His chickens were on a spit with several others. The smoke was delicious. The smell was lemon and garlic. Three young women looked at him but looked away. He felt completely immodest. The rented bathing suit had dried in an embarrassing shape. The three girls exchanged glances and smiles among themselves. Antonio started away, alerting Hovanes, as he passed, that he was going to the locker for his clothes.

When he returned, Ara introduced him to Annee and her cousins, who blushed, and so did he.

"So are my broders de best worker for you?" Annee asked.

"Yes."

"I'm glad. Where are you from?"

"Zacatecas."

"Where is dat?"

"Mexico. About a thousand miles from here."

"Whad is id like?"

"Mountains."

"You know Ararat?"

"No."

"Is Armenia mountain. Turks steal id. You know Nosark"

"No."

"From Bible, Nosark?"

"No."

"Animal," she made her fingers look like they were walking twoby-two, "animal, man-woman, Nosark, big flood."

"Oh yes, yes, Noah's Ark."

"Pieces of Nosark ship found on land on top of Mt. Ararat."

"I see, yes."

"Why you coming here?"

"Work."

"How about you?"

"Nothing left in Armenia for us. Turks killing our parents, grandparents, uncles, aunts."

"I'm sorry. Do you work?"

"Yes."

"What do you do."

"I work for studio."

"Movies?"

"Yes."

"You a star?"

Annee laughed. "Costume maker."

"That's wonderful."

"One minute,"she said. She walked away to go baste the chickens.

She came back with a cold bottle of beer for him. Nothing for herself.

Antonio could not sleep that night. He hadn't showered and still had salt on him from head to toe. But that wasn't it. He had Annee on his mind.

CHAPTER V

1929

IN 1929 A migrant foundry worker named Guillermo Vega attended the Cinco de Mayo celebration in Arroyo Bello. He did not play baseball. He watched the game, and drank.

When he spotted Beatriz, an unrelenting desire overtook him. He watched her closely. He watched her as he drank some more. He watched her after the baseball game when she joined with two boys. He watched the boys throw their gloves and bat down. He watched Beatriz and the boys stand in line together for food. He watched them eat.

When they finished eating the boys played catch in the dying light. A small Mariachi band played trumpets, violins, and two different sized guitars. Guillermo could wait no longer. He approached Beatriz and offered her some licorice and asked her if she had ever seen butterflies in the area. The little girl told him that she had but it was too cold for them now. "Show me where you saw them."

"All over here." "Down by the arroyo?"

"Yes."

"Show me."

"Sure."

Walking into the darkness he took her hand.

⚊⚊⚬⚊⚊

"Where were you?"

"A man took me to the arroyo."

"Who?"

"I don't know him." She began to cry.

"What happened?"

"He showed me his you know," she pointed to Leo's crotch, "and he put it in my mouth."

"What!" The act was unfathomable to the nine year olds. "Where is he now?"

"I don't see him. I ran away from him."

"Let's look." They picked up their things and made their way around the perimeter of the picnic.

"There he is." He sat, rocking on his haunches, near a car.

Leo came up to him. He looked at the young boy and at his two companions, instantly recognizing Beatriz. Leo belted him in the head with the baseball bat. The man swayed and reached for his skull. Leo belted him again. He toppled over.

"Let's go."

Beatriz's childhood was over. So was Leo's. And Eddy's too.

⋘⟨⟨●⟩⟩⋙

The railroad sent Pedro to Smithton's local doctor for a twisted ankle. Dr. Monson had an office in his house. Brick. Two stories. With a wide front porch. Pedro asked him if he owned the land around the house and the doctor said, "Yes."

Pedro asked him if he ever thought about doing some farming and suggested some good crops for the area, offering to grow them for the doctor. Pedro and his oldest boy could come on the weekend. Pedro and the doctor could split what they wanted for their own tables and sell the rest. The doctor agreed to a 75/25 split. The doctor would take the bigger share because it was his land and he would buy the seed.

The doctor's son, Avery, was also nine, the same age as Leo, Beatriz and Eddy. They had attended school together for four years. When Pedro and Leo went to the Monson place to plant crops, Leo was thrown together with Avery, a person with whom he had never associated at school.

"Hey Leo, let me show you something." The two boys wandered off from Pedro. They went into the house. The parlor was cool with big chairs, a sofa and several tables. A richly colored rug dominated the room. Lamps with lampshades and magazines on an end table caught

Leo's eye. It was a big house, dark inside except for concentrated rays of light, pouring through the windows, with dust particles in them. The house smelled faintly like lemon. No one was home.

When Dr. Monson returned, he went straight to his office. He found the boys trying to glue a broken bone from the skeleton that had stood on a rolling stand in the corner of his office.

Avery was not supposed to go into the office. Or touch anything. Enraged, but in a calm, yet stern, voice, Dr. Monson asked, "What's going on here?"

"Leo wanted to see the skeleton. He accidentally broke a rib."

Leo could not believe what he was hearing. Avery had yanked on the rib to bring the skeleton from the corner, but the roller on the bottom of the stand, stopped dead against an electrical cord, and the bone snapped off in Avery's hand.

"Is that true young man?" Dr. Monson towered over Leo glaring at him with piercing blue eyes, cold as scalpels.

Leo knew what it was like to have his own father mad at him. He looked at Avery, who was paralyzed with fear. "I'm sorry, Sir," copped Leo.

"Out with you both."

Dr. Monson pulled Pedro aside and told him what had happened. Pedro offered to pay for the skeleton.

"No. But I want you to reprimand your boy." And, he added, "He's not to set foot in the house again."

"Yes, Sir, Doctor Monson."

——•••——

When they sat in the truck, Pedro slapped Leo on the side of his head. "You know better. Why did you do it?"

"I didn't. Avery did."

"The doctor told me that you were the one who broke the skeleton."

"I told him I did."

"What's wrong with you?"

"But I didn't do it."

Pedro's frustration manifested itself in his right arm. He pulled it across his chest setting up an even stronger blow to the head of Leo.

"No, Papa. Here is what happened."

Pedro nodded to Leo to go ahead but held his arm in striking position for insurance in case he didn't like Leo's explanation.

"Avery took me into the house and showed me things. The skeleton was in the corner and he reached to pull it out. But the roller got caught on an electrical cord and the rib he was holding snapped off in his hand. That's all."

"So why did Dr. Monson tell me you did it?"

"Dr. Monson asked Avery what happened and Avery said I broke it. I looked at Avery and he looked real scared. I thought his father would let him have it so I said I did it."

"You didn't think his father would let you have it, did you?"

"I guess I didn't."

"Look. Don't get in a trap with these gringos where you have to count on them to get you out. They'll let you down. They think they're better than you."

"Aren't they?"

Pedro let his coiled hand fly against Leo's head. "I never want to hear anything like that from you. No one is better than you and no one is worse. Do you understand me?"

"I think so. But they're rich and we're poor. You are always yessiring everybody and nobody yes-sirs you back."

"I know. That's how it is. Someday. Maybe someday things will be different. I wouldn't work so hard and send you to school if I didn't think things could change. Look I don't want to hit you ever. You know that. So wise up."

"You are always telling me to wise up but I don't know what's wise or not."

"Just be a good kid and stay out of the gringos' way. Get an education and do something with your life."

Leo looked his father in the eye. His father meant what he was saying. They bounced along home in the truck. His father was wearing a red plaid flannel shirt, sleeves rolled up, blue and white neckerchief, dust-covered dungarees. His big hands moved from the steering wheel to the gear shift and back with ease. His worn work shoes worked the foot pedals. After a while his sour expression left him. He looked over without saying a word and smiled at Leo. He patted Leo's head. Pedro's big, thick mustache turned up and his thick shock of hair went waving in the breeze. Leo never forgot that picture of his father and was happy, after all, to have him back.

Leo had never liked Avery before, and never liked him since. Leo and Avery never talked about the skeleton. They kept a distance.

CHAPTER VI

1930

IN 1930 IN Los Angeles the Avakians bought a truck and started hauling trash on the weekends. They tried to get garbage routes and eventually succeeded. So they quit the Red Line. When they got up to three trucks they asked Antonio if he wanted to join them. And he did. For the next few years the business continued to grow. The Avakians worked hard and bought choice land in Montebello where they built a compound for their families.

At one of the usual Sunday gatherings at the compound, Antonio stopped by. He had made his way from the trucks to the front office and was running the paperwork side of the Avakian garbage business. Still shy, he only saw Annee infrequently at her family's gatherings. That evening she stood on the back patio with the distant lights of Los Angeles sparkling behind her.

"How have you been stranger?" she said.

"Good."

"My broders still de best worker for you?"

"Uh, I think it might be the other way around, now. How are you Annee?"

"I'm getting married."

"No, they didn't tell me."

"I told them not to. I wanted to tell you myself."

"Well, congratulations, who's the lucky guy?"

"Do you know Asadur Karabedian?"

"No."

"Well, it's him. He works for Edison. I've known him for years."

"That's great."

She smiled sadly, "Thanks."

After an awkward pause, she said, "I want to show you something. Come with me."

He followed her to her bungalow. Inside, faint odors of powder and perfume lingered. It was neat as a pin. She opened an armoire and took out a white dress that she held up.

"You'll make a beautiful bride," he said.

"You really think I'm beautiful?"

"I always did from the first."

"Why haven't you married and settled down?"

"I wanted to get ahead enough to feel comfortable in doing it."

"That's romantic." They laughed.

"Never met the right girl, huh?"

"No. Never saved enough money."

"So you have met the right girl?"

"I thought so, but ..."

"But what?"

"She's getting married."

They looked at each other for a moment. She tossed the dress atop the bed. They embraced.

"I love you Annee, but knowing your culture and your brothers, I could never ask you to marry me."

"Well, if you are asking, I'm accepting."

"Nothing could make me happier." They kissed.

They made their ways separately back to the patio. They exchanged glances and contemplated the pickle they were in. The brothers would be furious, not to mention Asadur.

⋯⟨⦿⟩⋯

"You are no longer part of this family. No longer Armenian. Are you out of your mind? Not going to marry Asadur. In love with Antonio." Ara could not get over his sister telling him she wanted to marry Antonio. Ara kept on her for a week. Her other brother, Hovanes, did not say a word.

Antonio told Ara and Hovanes that he wanted to speak to them. "I'm leaving," he said. "I'm sorry but I'll go look for a job. I love Annee."

"Go," Ara said.

That evening Ara knocked at Antonio's door. "Look. You partner. I don't want my sister marrying to bureaucrat. Come on. They're in the car. Let's celebrate." The brothers, their wives, Annee, and Antonio went to El Cholo Mexican restaurant on Western Avenue in LA for dinner, then on to the Seven Veils Club on Sunset Boulevard in Hollywood, to sit on the floor, watch belly dancing, and drink too much.

CHAPTER VII

1937

IN 1937, LEO'S high school baseball team did not lose a single regular season game, got to go to regionals for the first time, and won there. The State Championship would go to the team that won three tournament games in a row. It was single elimination. East High School from Salt Lake City had held the trophy for the last three years.

Leo pitched for Smithton. Eddy caught. The tournament was held at the baseball field at the University of Utah in Salt Lake City. Smithton was the unlikely opponent of East in the final game.

East had a pitcher six foot four, two hundred twenty pounds, with a blistering fastball, good for strikes and even better for moving and keeping hitters off the plate. The home plate umpire gave him a bigger strike zone than he gave Leo and constantly barked at Eddy to speak English, not "Mezcan," to his battery mate.

Going into the last inning, neither team had scored. Smithton's Gerald Reed, a huge ox and son of an alfalfa farmer, managed an opposite field single. Eddy came up and sacrifice-bunted him to second. One out. The next hitter struck out. Then Leo took his place in the batter's box. The first pitch was a brush-back aimed at his head. He figured the next for over the plate. He cracked it on a line into the gap for a double and Reed lumbered in, one to nothing. During the next at-bat, Leo stole third but was left stranded.

East was not going to give up the trophy easily and the meat of the batting order was coming up. Their first baseman led off, to be followed by the pitcher, and the third baseman. The first baseman was their best hitter, the number three spot in the lineup. He went after a fast ball but didn't get all of it. Smithton's Jerry Stubblefield played the ball, picking it clean to launch a throw from shortstop to first to mark the first out. The next batter, the pitcher, walked on four straight strikes and Eddy started jawing with the umpire.

Leo never expected anything from umpires and knew it would be this one's last chance to steer the game to East. He stood on the mound and looked over to the crowd. The bleachers were filled top to bottom with white faces. Except at the far end, a colorful little crowd of brown skinned people were hurling encouragement at him in Spanish. He narrowed his gaze to just Beatriz, whose lips he could read, *Vamos Leo! (Let's go Leo!).*

The next batter also walked. Leo called time and motioned Eddy over. "I'm going to end up walking in the winning run. You got to get these guys to swing."

"What can I do?"

"I don't know. Think of something."

The next batter settled in. "Hey batter. Hey." The batter would not acknowledge Eddy.

"Hey stupid. You can't hit. You got that dummy." The batter swung his bat at Eddy's head. The catcher's mask took the brunt of the wallop. The umpire awarded the batter first base for catcher's interference and told Eddy he would throw him out of the game if he heard another peep out of him – in any language.

Now what? Eddy thought to himself, shaking cobwebs from his head. Bases loaded, still one out.

Eddy had another idea. He called time, went to the mound and summoned the first baseman over. The Smithton coach did not want to waste a trip to the mound. He had every confidence in his boys, particularly Eddy. The inning before, a Pacific Coast League scout in the stands had told the Smithton coach that he was going to offer Leo a tryout after the game. The Smithton coach told him he should think about Eddy, too, for his baseball smarts.

"Look Carl," Eddy said to the first baseman, "we got to get them to swing. This umpire is calling all balls. Tell the runner on first he should have been kicked out of the game for coming at me with a bat and that East couldn't get a run across even on a bunt, but make real sure the first base coach hears what you tell him about bunting. Then play way back." Eddy called the third baseman over. "Look, you and Carl back way up, give them the bunt, Leo and I will cover it."

The next batter was a good bunter and a bunt was a good option. East's first base coach did not want to have the game end on a double play. He'd rather see the batter bunt than swing his way out of the championship. *One step at a time*, the coach was telling himself. He had no idea the home plate ump was on his side and he just wanted to get the game tied. *Why not bunt? No one was hitting off the Mexican, anyway.*

The first base coach overheard what Carl had to say about bunting and saw Carl playing back. The first base coach glanced at the third baseman who was also playing way back. It was a golden opportunity. The first base coach gave the bunt sign. The batter laid down a bunt that bounced chest high off home plate, fair. Eddy grabbed it bare-handed out of the air, dragged his foot across home plate for a force out, then threw a strike to Carl at first for the game-ending double play. Score the play two-three. Smithton was victorious.

No sooner were Smithton's players leaping for joy when East's pitcher, who had taken off from third on the pitch, barreled full speed into Eddy, whose back had been turned. Eddy went flying, crashing head first into the steel corner of the backstop. Leo got to him right away. Eddy had a huge purple bleeding bump on his forehead but a smile on his face as he heaved himself to his feet.

Leo looked over at East's pitcher who sneered back and said, "That stupid Mexican was in my way." East's pitcher had fifty pounds on Leo. Still Leo went at him and beat him to within an inch of his life.

The officials awarded the game to East for Smithton's unsportsmanlike conduct.

⸻ ◦《◉》◦ ⸻

Pedro hounded Leo all the way back from Salt Lake City for letting those gringos take the championship away from him. "It was your fault. You had it and you blew it."

"It's not fair, Papa."

Leo did not get the tryout from the Pacific Coast League scout either. Not because of the scout, but because of the owner, the scout had called, to report on Leo's pitching and *hitting* performance.

Eddy's face ballooned. The rest of him ached along with his swollen face for days.

Beatriz ignored the result of the ballgame – proud as could be for both Leo and Eddy.

The school suspended Leo for two days for fighting, and Eddy played hooky with him. The two went fishing for catfish at a pond near Santaquin.

It was a lazy spring day with temperatures more like summer than spring.

"I don't get it. We beat those guys. We were undefeated and we still lose.That pitcher had no reason to level you. I try to make things square and they take everything from us."

"Don't worry, Leo, we'll get them next year."

"I ain't playin' next year."

"Come on, Leo. We'll win state. We can do it again." Leo would not comment.

Eddy changed the subject to the upcoming prom. "Say, you going to the prom?"

"Can we?"

"So far as I know it's not '*Mexicanos prohibidos*.' But it cost $10 to go and everyone knows we don't have that kind of money to spend on a prom. I wanted to take Beatriz."

Eddy had been in love with Beatriz since first grade. Leo fell for her the day of the picnic. Because only Eddy would talk about how he felt about Beatriz, Leo, loyal to his friend, never spoke a word.

"I'll give you ten bucks if you want to go."

"Come on, Leo, you don't have ten bucks."

"I sure do. My dad gives me a share of the crops from the Monson place."

"When could I pay you back? It would take me forever."

"Pay me when you can."

＊＊＊

"Beatriz, listen, I've been thinking about the prom, ah, would you like to go with me?"

"Eddy?" She gave him a quizzical look like he had to be joking.

"I mean it. You want to go?"

"Why didn't you ask me before?"

"What do you mean. Leo is going to lend me the ten dollars. I just found out."

"Leo?"

"Yeah."

"Is he taking someone?"

"No. He's not going."

"Oh."

Eddy looked at her. Her face previewed some bad news. "I can't. Avery Monson asked me."

"What?"

"Yeah. He asked me yesterday. My mom told me to go with him."

"What about your dad?"

"Well, you know, he's been out of work for a long time and drinking, I couldn't really ask him. My mom told me to go with him."

"Do you want to go with him?"

"I'd rather go with you."

"Then tell him *No.*"

"I can't. I already told him *Yes.*"

⚯

The night of the prom Avery picked Beatriz up in his father's Buick. It was shiny, black, clean and polished, spotless, at least before it made its way through a gorge and down a gully into the shanty town where Beatriz lived. Her mother was all nerves waiting for the boy and quarreling with her husband to put a shirt on before the Buick showed up.

Beatriz wore a pale yellow dress made from shiny fabric. Her mother had dyed her sister's wedding dress and taken in the skirt.

Eddy and Leo lurked at the scene of Beatriz's departure from the corner of Eddy's house. They toted several bottles of beer that they would drink on the long stroll to the school's gym where they would stay outside and listen to the band, hoping that Beatriz would break free for a moment and come say *Hello.* They wanted to see her dressed up, up close. From afar she made a golden goddess. The face and its beautifully carved features rivaled Dolores Del Rio's that night. The boys watched her glide like a movie star in a sound studio from a shabby western set right into a sleek black sedan. And even though neither of the boys was taking her they were happy for her that she was going. Avery — to the extent they thought about him at all — was a minor annoyance.

—⊶«◉»⊷—

When the band took a break Beatrice wandered outside the gym. Coming up to Leo and Eddy she said, "I wish you two were inside."

She was too much a vision to them for them to get words out. "What's wrong? Cat's got your tongue?" she added.

Each boy was trying to compose something clever. The problem was she was simply overwhelming in her demeanor and looks. They had never seen her so radiant. Or maybe they had never loved her so much.

Eddy finally said, "Is he treating you nice?"

"He's OK." Beatriz didn't tell them how he pressed real close to her and kept looking down her dress.

"Well," said Eddy, "he better behave or Leo will bounce a baseball bat off his head."

Immediately as he said it he felt awful. The three of them were stunned into silence. They had never talked about it. Ever. It had always been their secret. Eddy didn't know where that came from. "I'm sorry."

"Never mind." More silence. She looked at Leo and wished she were dancing with him. "OK, I got to go." She turned and left.

"I'm so stupid," Eddy said, making a face.

"It's OK. Let's go home." That conversation and the walk home left them sober. They raided Leo's mom's kitchen for food and went down the gorge to watch the nighttime sky, listen for creatures, and make sure Beatriz got back all right.

—⊶«◉»⊷—

Avery drove short of the gorge, stopped the car and pulled on the hand brake. Its teeth made a clicking sound. Beatriz felt trapped. Avery leaned to kiss her. She said *No*. He reached for her shoulder and dragged his hand down the front of her dress. "No, no," she insisted, pushing his hand away. Avery sat back, seething. He slapped her across the face, undid the hand brake, started the car, and peeled out. There was a jog in the road ahead, down to the right and up to the left. The car was going too fast to take it. The car flipped on its side and Beatriz bumped her head against the steel bar between the front and back doors.

***

Leo and Eddy had fallen asleep. Instead of being awakened by the Monson car it was Beatriz's mother, on foot, who came upon them. "Boys, have you seen Beatriz?"

"Isn't she back yet?"

"No. I'm worried."

"Don't worry, I'll get my dad's truck and we'll go look for her."

Just before the gorge was the Monson car on its side. Beatriz had been pulled clear and lay dead. Avery had left her to hike home.

Leo and Eddy found her. Eddy carefully gathered her into his arms. He clung to her body in the cab of the truck as Leo drove. They took the body into the house. Beatriz' father broke down. Neighbors gathered outside. Her mother blamed herself. They called the Sheriff. Eddy was crying inconsolably. Leo tried to comfort him but Eddy pushed him away. "Leave me alone."

Eddy went to get his .22 rifle and he was going after Avery.

The Sheriff picked up Avery and drove him home to consult with his father before going out to the gully where the Mexicans lived. The Sheriff took Dr. Monson along with him to examine the girl. She was laid out in her prom dress on her parent's bed. Hands folded. Eyes closed. Not a mark on her, except a reddened cheek, and the bruise on her temple. Dr. Monson emerged from the bed room, "Thin skull. She must have had a thin skull. It was an accident. I drove through the gorge by the accident scene. The road there is unsafe at any speed. It's a shame."

The Sheriff chimed in, "Yeah, you know, let's get a crew out there and do something with the road."

Dr. Monson inoculated the mother and father and a few others to calm them down.

The local telephone operator got a call from Avery Monson. She went to the Sheriff's office and rang him on the two-way radio in his car to relay what Avery had said. One of the Mexican kids milling about near the Sheriff's car heard the operator's call come in. The kid ran and got the Sheriff. The Sheriff came out and called back on his radio. He got the operator. She told him that Avery Monson had called and said Eddy Velasco was calling him out of his house and Eddy had a gun.

The Sheriff sped off with the doctor.

Eddy stood there demanding that Avery come out and tell him what happened. Avery told him to go away, it was an accident. The Sheriff pulled up and said, "What have you got there? Is that a rifle?"

Of course it was. Eddy held the end of the barrel, resting it against his leg. He hadn't pointed it at Avery and wasn't going to use it. Eddy threw it aside. The Sheriff walked up and cuffed him. Eddy spent the rest of the night in jail. Next morning he learned that Dr. Monson was pressing assault charges and wanted him kept locked up so he couldn't menace Avery.

Leo was allowed a few minutes with Eddy. Leo told Eddy that Beatriz's funeral was the next day.

The Sheriff decided to keep Eddy locked up for the funeral and talked to an Army recruiter about taking the boy.

Beatriz was buried. Eddy went into the Army. And Leo brooded with the rest of the Mexican families.

Nothing happened to Avery.

When Leo heard Avery bragging to another classmate about his sexual conquest of Beatriz he walked up to Avery and told him to meet him after school at the arroyo at 4 o'clock.

At precisely that hour the Sheriff pulled next to the arroyo and rolled down his window.

"Leo, that was a great game you pitched against East High." "Thanks."

The Sheriff got out of his car and lit a cigarette.

"Leo, I wanted to do what I thought was best for Eddy. I didn't want to see him get in trouble."

Leo looked over at the arroyo, running high from the winter snows, thinking ahead to the annual picnic and back to that night with the baseball bat, and Beatriz.

"Look son, you can't solve problems with violence. Avery's a worthless bastard but his dad runs things around here. Do me a favor and keep away from him."

"My dad's advice, the first day I went to the Monson's."

"Yeah, how's your dad?"

"He's good. The same. My dad never changes."

"He's a good man. You know, let's go over to your house I need to have a talk with him. Come on, son. I don't need to tell you, you're wasting your time if you think Avery will show up here today in response to your invitation," the Sheriff cackled before adding, "polite as it may have been."

Pedro's house was the biggest in the gully. The best kept. And remarkably quiet for housing the most kids. Pedro was not happy to see the Sheriff's car arrive with Leo in it.

"Pedro."

"Sheriff. What's he done?"

"Nothing. I just gave him a ride. You know he's a hell of a ballplayer."

"Yes. Too bad he lost the State Championship with fighting."

"It wasn't fair," said the Sheriff.

"No. But it happened."

"Next year. We'll get'm next year."

"Not without Eddy," Leo chimed in. "Catcher is the most important position on the team."

The Sheriff disagreed, "You can't win without pitching."

"You can't win without nine guys but catcher is still the most important position on a baseball team."

"How can you be so sure, Leo?"

"Because Eddy told me that every day of his life." They laughed.

"Like some coffee, Sheriff?"

"Yes, I would."

"Come on in."

Teresa put together a tray with coffee and *pan dulce* (pastry).

"Tell me, Pedro, what is Leo going to do after high school?"

"They'll take him on the railroad."

"That sounds great." The Sheriff realized from one look over to Leo that Leo did not share his enthusiasm.

"How 'bout you, son? Looking forward to the railroad."

"If it helps the family, sure."

The Sheriff noticed two Colt .45s mounted on the wall.

"That's quite a pair, Pedro. Where'd you get those?"

"Well, from my father."

"Geez. Was he a gunslinger?"

"No. Just a farmer. He got them from some bounty hunters."

"A gift?"

"No. More like a reminder."

"How so?"

"A reminder not to mess with my mother."

"The plot thickens."

"The bounty hunters went after my mother and she defended herself. When the dust settled, she had hacked one up with a machete and shot the other two."

"She go to jail?"

"No. No one ever found out."

The Sheriff took a long sip of coffee trying to figure out how to dismiss his obligations as an officer of the court and an enforcer of the law.

"Both your parents gone now, Pedro?"

"They died of typhoid fever when I was eleven."

"Oh. Sorry."

Leo wondered why he had never heard that story from his father before.

"So," the Sheriff asked, "is there a third gun?"

"Yes, I use it for target practice."

"Can I see it?"

"Sure." Pedro went out of the room and returned shortly.

"Wow, that's a beauty! Is it accurate?"

"About as accurate as I am." They laughed.

"It's not loaded?"

"Not now."

Pedro could see how much joy the pistol gave the Sheriff as he held it and examined it.

"How do you like it?"

"It's great. Would you ever consider parting with it?"

"I never thought about it."

"I mean for a good price."

"No. I wouldn't sell it, but seeing how much you admire it, I'd give it to you."

The generosity of the response jarred the Sheriff. It made him think twice about asking to buy such a cherished memento.

"No, look, I'm glad you let me see it. Maybe someday we can go shooting. But I wouldn't take it as a gift, and you're right, you shouldn't sell it either, no, thanks for showing it to me, that's quite a collection. Your mother must have been quite a woman."

Pedro, as if eleven again, pictured her in his mind's eye and nodded.

⸻ ((◉)) ⸻

Pedro got a letter from Antonio announcing the birth of his third child. Pedro wrote back, told him he'd never catch up, and stuck a ten-dollar bill in the envelope "for college."

Leo went to his father in August and told him he wanted a job on the railroad and he did not want to finish school. "That job will always be there. Get your education."

"I don't need it for the railroad. Do you think they'd take me over a White high school graduate when time came for a promotion?"

"No, you're right. Say, have you heard anything from Eddy?"

"He's in El Paso, Texas, at Fort Bliss. He's taking classes to finish High School and he is trying to get into the Navy."

"Can he do that?"

"You know Eddy, he thinks he can do anything."

"Leo, please finish school. You are still young. June is not that far off. If you were working like me you'd think it was coming too soon. Finish for your mom, Eddy, Beatriz, this whole damn gully, we never had a high school graduate before."

"OK, Pop."

"And play baseball."

⸻ ((◉)) ⸻

Leo did both but the team didn't make it to regionals. After the deciding game, the Sheriff went up to Leo and said, "Great year, Leo — if only we had catching."

Leo graduated and went to work for the railroad. The railroad boss hounded and rode Leo every chance he got.

Late one night, Pedro lay in bed with Teresa. "Teresa, what should we do?"

"About what?"

"It's Leo. The boss is riding him worse than any new man I've ever seen. Leo's smart and strong and does a real good job. He doesn't deserve what he's getting."

"Can't you do anything for him?"

"That's just it. If I try, they'd probably fire the both of us."

"I wish Leo had a girl," Teresa said.

"He never got over Beatriz."

"But she was Eddy's girl. That's what Leo told me."

"You were talking to the wrong person, Teresa. Ever see Beatriz with the two of them. She loved Leo and he loved her. That's it."

"You give him too much credit sometimes."

"He needs all he can get. Do you know how tough it is to always get shortchanged because you're not White?"

"Who do you think you are talking to, Pedro? Listen, what about your friend Antonio, out in California, maybe he can help Leo get started. I would hate for Leo to go, but he'll end up like you if he stays."

Truth never hurt Pedro. He didn't get angry with Teresa. He knew she was guileless and honestly blunt. There was no malice in what she had told him. Anyway, down deep, he wanted the best for his kids — a life different from his.

CHAPTER VIII

1939

ANTONIO MET LEO at Union Station on Alameda Street in Los Angeles. "You know you look a lot like your dad. A lot like him the last time I saw him, in fact."

"My dad sends best regards."

"So what do you think about picking up garbage."

"Well," Leo paused, "I need a job."

"When I started years ago, we used to say it was a great job. Ten dollars a week and all the leftovers you could eat."

They both laughed.

Leo started to work the next day. It was a hot Los Angeles morning. The limpid air would turn into peach colored smog by day's end. Urban, residential, and vacant patches of land were scattered along straight and lengthy boulevards. Brick and stone buildings in the downtown area were surrounded by stucco and wooden houses and hotels. The earthy patches of ground were sun-hardened clay, a color lighter than sand. There were more people and cars in five square blocks than in all of Smithton.

Corner news barkers shouted, "Extra! Extra! Get your Times, Germany invades Poland." Leo had thought seriously about joining up. He was waiting to hear from Eddy to see if Eddy was staying in the Army or going in the Navy. In any event, Leo, for the immediate future, found himself a garbage man. Not too glamorous. "But necessary for the common good," he told himself. The job was six days a week and it kept him in great physical shape.

On Sunday he hob-knobbed with Antonio, his family, and the other owners of the business, Ara and Hovanes. Ara threw barbecues at his big, beautiful house, and lots of people came. They played volleyball on grass in the massive back yard. Chess and backgammon games abounded for the less physically, more mentally inclined. Armenian predominated, followed by broken English. Leo was in the minority with his unaccented, fluent English. The barbecued chicken, lamb and beef kebab were out of this world, along with the *dolma* (stuffed grape leaves). He loved all the new taste delights, including *hummus* and a salad made of tomatoes, cucumbers and onions, with a lemon and vinegar dressing. Most of all he liked the fact that it was all he could eat.

Leo had lettered in football, basketball, baseball and track but had never picked up a volleyball. It didn't matter. He learned to bump, set, serve, dig and spike, and he was a natural leaper. Within a short time he was one of the best on the court.

He met a number of girls near his age at the barbecues, though none interested him.

⸺◉⸺

One Friday afternoon Antonio was under the gun, reconciling the books for the garbage business. He would be late picking up Annee so he let Leo off early to go pick her up at Paramount Studios on Melrose Avenue. She had a crew of five seamstresses working under her.

The sewing machines were humming at flank speed when Leo found his way to Annee. One of the girls caught his eye. She glanced over, unshy about taking him in. It would be several months before he would see her again, when he tagged along with Antonio and Annee, to a wrap party for "Mr. Smith Goes to Washington."

Her name was Rosa Mejia. She was nineteen. Illegal. Prior work experience, prostitution. She had left Tijuana two years before.

She walked up to Leo at the studio party. "You're the boy who picked up Annee." Her English, in terms of grammar, and lack of a Mexican accent, was uncannily good. She was one of those people who had an ear for languages.

"Yes."

"You're not Armenian?"

"No. I'm Mexican, but born in Colorado."

"I'm from Guadalajara," she lied.

"I've never been to Mexico."

"I'll never go back," she told the truth. "Well what do you think of all this?"

"It's nice. I was brought up in a small town. LA is an amazing place. Seeing movie stuff back stage is great."

"What is the name of the small town?"

"Smithton, in Utah."

"Utah? You moved there from Colorado?"

"Yes."

"What's it like?"

"Hot in the summer, cold in the winter, a lot of snow, not like here."

"Mountains?"

"Yes. I lived next to the Wasatch Mountains."

"How do you like the ocean?"

"I haven't been yet."

"You're kidding!"

"No. I'm not."

"Annee will take you. She and her husband took us in July. Maybe in a few months when it warms up, they'll take you."

"When you say took us, who was that?"

"The girls who work with her."

"Oh. Is she a good boss?"

"The best. And a great teacher. I used to help my mom sew (a lie), but I've learned so much more from Annee." Actually, Rosa, having clothes ripped off of her in Tijuana by overzealous johns, was led by necessity to needle and thread.

Antonio interrupted the conversation. "Hello, Rosa," he said flatly, "Leo," he commanded, "we're leaving now." Leo said good-bye to the young seamstress and said maybe he'd see her again. She nodded and smiled.

Pedro turned forty. There was a big party for him at the arroyo. Leo sent him a package with a Pendleton shirt in it. A red plaid virgin wool shirt, perfect for the cool evening. A step up from his usual flannels. He wore it proudly. Everyone missed Leo. His younger brothers and sisters, his mom, but no one more than Pedro. The sheriff cruised by the arroyo to tone down the drinking and asked after Leo. "He's a garbage man in Los Angeles," Pedro said.

"I guess he'll never run out of work," quipped the Sheriff.

"Don't worry. He'll get on with life, maybe meet the right girl. You know."

"Yeah, Pedro, we'll see what happens to this lot. I think they're all headed to war," said the Sheriff.

"Me, too." That reminded Pedro. "Oh, Eddy is in the Navy, down in San Diego. He and Leo are getting together once Eddy finishes training."

"That's great. Those two boys are something special."

Leo left on the morning train for San Diego. The train hissed and jerked, tugging slowly into motion from next to a platform, gaining speed in the train yard, picking up pace, clicking and clacking to the edge of the city, then, rambling smoothly through the countryside, past little farms, empty lands, oil derricks, and on to the coast. It stopped at places with Spanish names. Santa Ana, a sleepy place with washed out colors and dry air. San Juan Capistrano, the site of an old Spanish mission, sunny, bright, with colorful flowers clinging next to the tracks and perfuming the air for each visiting train car. And, San Clemente, a little beach town next to a big blue ocean.

From there, the train hugged the coast, rattling freely for much of an hour, stopping at Del Mar, before reaching San Diego, smaller than LA, sitting at the side of a bay. The sights, sounds and speed of travel had exhilarated Leo, adding to the excitement of seeing Eddy again.

Eddy was wearing Navy whites, not the blue uniform on the Cracker Jack box that Leo had envisioned. Eddy was older, taller. More muscular. Not the same skinny kid who would take on all comers at home plate and bounce back up.

Leo and Eddy shook hands and said some awkward things to each other, acting uncomfortably formal for two kids who had grown up together and shared so much. Immediately, Eddy suggested going to a bar on Broadway to have a beer. Leo was reluctant because he was underage. Eddy believed the uniform would get the two of them served without any questions.

"Let's take in some sights first and we can go there later," Leo suggested.

They wandered several blocks toward the bay, gazed across at Coronado, up to Point Loma and down to Mexico. They ate seafood at a market near the fishing boats and talked about what they were doing.

They made their way back to Broadway and the "Seven Seas Bar," got carded, and were refused service. But the bartender gave them directions to a Mexican restaurant only a few blocks away, where they were served.

They wondered aloud when the US would get involved in the war. Leo reminded Eddy that the US had stayed out of the first world war for nearly two years before getting into it. Eddy said it could be a matter of days, weeks, or months before the US got in. But getting in was a sure bet. Everyone he knew had a different opinion on timing but agreed completely on involvement.

Eddy wanted to see action but was relieved that he was headed in the other direction for now. He left the Army for the Navy because he hated the marching, standing in line, and his Drill Sergeant, most of all, because the Drill Sergeant called all the Latinos, wetbacks. In the Navy, Eddy had qualified for the engine room.

Eddy told Leo about his Army Drill Sergeant. At graduation, when Army basic training was over, the Drill Sergeant told Eddy he knew how much Eddy hated him, so much that Eddy would come back some day just to piss on the Drill Sergeant's grave.

"You're wrong, Drill Sergeant, Sir" Eddy told him, "I've had enough standing in line for a lifetime."

It had taken the Drill Sergeant a little while to get what Eddy had said, but Leo got it in no time.

——◄(●)►——

Leo got back late to LA and did not look forward to getting up in a few hours. On the train ride back he thought about Eddy. The boy was not over Beatriz, and searching, it seemed, for meaning in a life that had come apart at the seams only a few years before. Leo thought both he and Eddy would end up fighting the Germans even though Eddy was headed for Hawaii.

——◄(●)►——

"Leo?" Annee called.

"Time to get up."

"I'm up."

"Leo, how is your friend?"

"He's good, I guess."

"What do you mean, you guess?" Annee had a way of prying things out of Leo like no one else could.

"Just...some people don't get over things. He's one of them."

"What was it."

"There was a girl. She died in a car wreck on prom night."

"Your friend was driving?"

"No."

"Oh. Sorry. Well please hurry, Leo. I've got breakfast ready."

"Thanks, Annee."

She paused a moment longer. "Leo, you weren't the driver?"

"Oh, no."

"How about you, did you get over it?"

"Nope."

"Leo," she paused, "Rosa has asked me about you. Would you like me to invite her this Sunday to my brother's barbeque?"

Leo laughed. "I don't know."

"Then, I will."

——◄(●)►——

The road to the dump was dead straight and flat as can be. It was made of concrete, laid down in 150 foot sections. One day Leo found a shoe box filled with old golf balls while picking up the Municipal Golf Courses in Griffith Park. He rode shotgun on the way to the dump and tried his hand at hitting signs and trees along the way with the discarded golf balls. It was the pitcher in him.

On one throw, a wooden sign shot the ball back onto the road and the ball bounced against the hood of the truck. Doink. There was probably a dent in the hood. But the ball shot off the truck, bounced forward, and hit the truck, or the truck hit it, a second time. The truck was doing about 35 miles an hour. Bedros, the driver, and Leo were laughing their heads off at what had happened. Leo launched another ball into the middle of the lane ahead. Sure enough the ball bounced up, hit the truck, bounced forward, and the process repeated three more times in all before the ball bounced away at an angle off the truck and over to the side of the road.

Leo threw another ball into the road ahead. It bounced up and both Leo and Bedros started to duck. Smack. In the blink of an eye the windshield of the truck was all cracked. Leo and Bedros looked at each other with mouths wide and eyes popping. After a short pause they began to laugh nervously at their good fortune to have survived.

When they got back to the yard they told Antonio that kids had thrown rocks at them from an overhead bridge — and he bought it.

⸺⸺◉⸺⸺

Rosa had fled Tijuana. At sixteen she had found work dancing in a club called the Tin-Tin on Revolucion Avenue. She wanted to make money fast and go to America. At first it seemed everyone was protective of her but soon she was on her own and expected to do a lot worse things than dance.

She plotted with a girlfriend, Carmen, to leave. Their plan met fruition after they met a coyote (smuggler) who stashed them under the back seat of a '34 Oldsmobile and drove them across the border. They had to pay him fifty dollars apiece, and have sex with him, both at the same time, in advance. Once in Los Angeles, Rosa tried to dance in movies. That did not work out but she was able to get into the costume department. Her friend Carmen became a waitress.

Antonio did not like Annee's matchmaking, particularly Leo with Rosa. He had heard the other girls talk about her. While he did not have the complete story, he had enough to place her on Tijuana's strip of night clubs where anything went. Leo, Antonio thought, could do much better with an Armenian girl and gain an inside track into the business office.

Leo asked Rosa out after seeing her at the Sunday barbeque at Ara's. Leo asked her if she wanted to see *The Wizard of Oz* at the Pantages Theater in Hollywood. She did. She told him that she and Annee had worked for MGM on the film and she had met Harold Arlen who wrote the "Rainbow" tune for the movie. She had also met Arlen's wife, a beautiful girl, along with Ray Bolger, and Munchkins aplenty.

Leo walked out of the theater after the movie agreeing with Dorothy. There's no place like home. He found the movie entertaining. A short break from the realities of the day.

They strode along Hollywood Boulevard toward Highland. Rosa wore a gabardine off-white dress, navy gloves, hat and shoes. Leo could not help but compare her to Beatriz. Rosa moved with the same grace, but laughed more easily. Both Beatriz and Rosa could devour him with their eyes. Rosa thought about bringing Leo to her apartment but hesitated. Her instincts told her no. She would go slow with him.

Rosa lived on Grace Street just above Franklin Avenue in Hollywood in a studio apartment she shared with Carmen, who had found a job in a restaurant on Beverly Boulevard, ironically, she thought, named *El Coyote*. It was owned by a very nice white lady, Mrs. Manning, who had come to Los Angeles from Oklahoma during the depression; and it was run by a man, whose sexual preferences pleased Carmen a great deal. He left all the waitresses alone. He wanted the bus boys instead.

After Tijuana, Carmen wanted nothing more to do with men. She only wanted Rosa but never said or did anything to encourage it. She knew she could not change Rosa's nature any more than she could change her own.

Still Carmen would listen for the faucet in the shower to shut off and catch glimpses of Rosa coming out of the bathroom, naked, or in a towel, giving Carmen an image to take with her to bed.

"It's not that easy, Antonio. These goddamn Russians are getting the new routes. We need someone at City Hall." Ara wanted to grow the business.

They found someone at City Hall for a price. Robert Entwhistle was twenty-six years old. From Beverly Hills. His parents owned a hanger factory and supplied most of the hangers in Los Angeles to the department stores, dry cleaners, and studios. They had contracts with every branch of service from San Francisco to San Diego. Entwhistle's father had political clout. He was a big contributor in every election.

Entwhistle's father got him on the City Council despite the boy's lack of experience and playboy lifestyle. Entwhistle had graduated from USC near the bottom of his class, drove a snazzy car, and did nothing but chase girls and booze it up.

He had the swing vote on the City Council that the Avakians needed if they were going to continue to compete in the sanitation business.

Hovanes handed Entwhistle $50,000 cash stuffed into a money vest during one of Entwhistle's dinner dates with a promising young starlet at the Brown Derby, passing the vest underhanded from one stall to the next in the Men's Room there.

The Avakians got only one new route for it, which hadn't been the deal — they were promised two — and Entwhistle wanted more money for future routes. Ara was furious with Entwhistle and his tantrums showed it. Hovanes was too, but no one could ever read what he was feeling.

Leo was promoted to driver.

CHAPTER IX

1941

ARA THREW A huge 4th of July party at the family compound that included fireworks. The day was miserably hot and exceptionally humid. The afternoon grew suffocatingly hotter when what little breeze there had been died down. Mid-afternoon Leo found Antonio sweltering over a game of chess and told him he was off to an air-conditioned movie with Rosa. "Ara will not like it," Antonio warned.

"OK, I'll talk to him."

Ara was fine with the idea and said he only wished he were going with them.

After leaving the party Rosa said, "Let's skip the movie and go to the beach. We can stay for the fireworks."

"Sure."

They took a taxi from Ara's to Santa Monica Boulevard in Hollywood and a trolley the rest of the way to the Santa Monica pier. They rented bathing suits and joined the throngs in the water. Finally they felt cool and refreshed. They went in and out of the water all afternoon and into the dusky evening before returning the bathing suits and changing back into their summer clothes.

For the sunset a great red ball above the horizon dropped slowly into a shiny pink ocean in dying light.

The fireworks were brilliant, shot from the pier and reflected over the water. The crowds oohed and aahed.

Most people left when the fireworks ended.

Rosa and Leo lingered at the beach. They took the last two hot dogs slathered in mustard from a beach vendor. The young couple walked past others snuggling on beach blankets in the sand. Waves crashed in the distance and light from a sliver of moon was dancing on the water and keeping pace with Leo and Rosa every step of their stroll.

Once they were all alone, Rosa said, "I want to go back in."

Leo just looked at her. She took off her blouse and skirt, darting into the ocean in bra and panties. He sat down, watched her frolic, and surveyed the beach up and down for any sign of life. It was quiet. No one was around. She came out and stood in front of him. She took off the wet underwear. He could only make out her form. She looked surreal – moonlit with water droplets. She lowered herself onto him and he held her tightly. They made love.

Rosa woke Carmen about 12:30 a.m. and told her she was in love. Carmen groggily agreed and hopelessly wished Rosa would take a pass on the details.

⸺ ((◉)) ⸺

Rosa missed her period. In discussions with Carmen, Rosa told her she did not want to go back to Tijuana for what would be her second abortion.

"You've got to talk to him," Carmen confided.

⸺ ((◉)) ⸺

Ara had tried in vain to get Robert Entwhistle to come for a Sunday barbecue. Ara needed Entwhistle's attention and to float a plan that Ara believed could work for the both of them. Entwhistle finally agreed to accept Ara's invitation to come to his house. It was for the first Sunday in October.

Entwhistle wanted to leave the moment he arrived. He found the Avakian compound ostentatious and bizarre, out of place anywhere, but especially in such a rundown part of town. The hilltop view did not approach the ones in the canyons above Hollywood or Beverly Hills or off Sunset Boulevard on the west side. These people, Entwhistle arrogantly concluded, were the immigrants his father kept warning him about. They were not going back to the strange sounding places they had come from. Particularly, now they had money.

So taking it from them made Entwhistle feel downright patriotic. Ara and Hovanes met with Entwhistle in the library. They drank Armanac out of snifters and smoked Havanas, the best money could buy.

By mistake, Rosa, also a guest that evening, walked into the library. The men stood up.

"Oh, I'm sorry. I was looking for the kitchen."

"To the right down the hall, through the dining room and you are there," said Ara.

Rosa thanked him and left. "Who is she?" asked Entwhistle.

"A seamstress, works with my sister at the studios in the costume departments."

"Mexican?"

"Yes."

"Is she legal?"

"I'm sure she is."

"So, if I understand this correctly, you want to give me a percentage of what you make, rather than pay me whatever I ask for a route, is that it?"

"Yes."

"And how long did you say this percentage will last?"

"Two years on each route."

"That's not a very long time."

"But LA growing. The city needing new routes all the time."

"Five years."

Ara looked at Hovanes, who remained expressionless, then looked back at Entwhistle. Ara forced a smile and held out his hand.

⊜

Rosa had been looking for Leo when she happened into the library where Entwhistle was meeting with the Avakians. She found Leo outside on a darkened patio gazing at city lights. The two of them had been together a few more times after the 4th of July. His head was wound tight with her, the war in Europe, and whether she might be pregnant.

She broke the ice. "Leo, I need to tell you something." He just looked at her and waited.

"I'm pregnant."

"Have you been to a doctor."

"No. But I am."

The reality of what she was saying had a strange effect on him. First of all, thinking she might be pregnant was a whole lot different than hearing her say it. Second, it gave him an instant erection. *True love*, he thought.

"Well?" she asked.

"I don't know what to say." He meant it in a most positive way. But she didn't take it that way. She wanted him to take her in his arms.

He just stood there with a hidden hardon.

"Leo," she said disappointedly, "You think about it, OK?"

"Yes, I will."

She walked away.

He intended to follow her into the light once his pants fit better. But she went into the house and called a cab from a phone in the hall. Then she went straight to the street, without a word to anyone.

Robert Entwhistle met her again at the front of the property and asked her if she needed a lift.

"No, thank you, I am waiting for a cab."

"No bother. Get in." He was a very pretty gringo and persuasive at that. During the drive, he made up an excuse to stop at his apartment off Third Street before dropping her in Hollywood. He invited her up. She reluctantly agreed. Half curious, half depressed, at that point.

He offered her a drink. He was already tipsy. She declined but he insisted. He served her Amaretto. "You have to sniff it first." Sweet vapors with an almond aroma. She liked it.

She had a second one. "I really must get home. I have to be up early tomorrow. I start at 8 o'clock at the studio."

"Are you a friend of Ara?" he asked.

"Not really. I work for his sister, Annee. Do you know her."

"No. I haven't had the pleasure."

"Do you trust Ara?" Entwhistle asked.

"I don't know what you mean."

"Ever done any business with him?"

"Oh, no."

"I see."

He bent his head closer to her. "You know you are a beautiful girl."

"I'm engaged."

"Oh, you are?"

"Yes," she lied again.

"Well where is your fiancé?"

"He's in the Army."

"Oh. Where is he stationed?"

"In San Diego."

"Oh, I bet you miss him?"

"Yes."

"Look Rosa. It is Rosa, isn't it?"

"Yes."

"You ever been with a man?"

She didn't look shocked and she didn't slap his face. Her expression was giving her away. She looked down.

Entwhistle pounced on her. She gave up after a brief skirmish, convinced he would smack her around if he did not get his way. *Just another drunken gringo to add to a long list,* she rationalized. She was still mad at Leo.

Entwhistle called a cab when he was done and gave her a few extra dollars over cab fare.

—⟩⟨⟨•⟩⟩⟨—

Leo called her at the studio the next day and made a date with her for Friday night.

"Look, I've been thinking. I want to marry you. I don't have enough money now, I don't know what's going to happen. I might get drafted. I might go somewhere and never make it back."

It didn't bother her that the proposal was wishy-washy. It was something else.

"Leo, you never said you loved me."

He looked at her. He'd never said the words, until now, "Rosa, I love you."

She hugged him. They went to a rundown hotel and made love. After they made love, she told him about Robert Entwhistle raping her.

Leo wanted to kill him. But he was not going to let his temper get the best of him and have another gringo ruin his life. He would get the authorities involved. He took Rosa, over her very strong protests, to the local police station.

Leo and Rosa waited a long time without being helped. When someone finally saw them and the story came out, they were told to drop it.

The police officer interviewing them realized they were talking about the City Councilman. The cop would never report her to INS, but to get her to drop the charges, he asked her if she was legal, intimating that she could be deported, and also made it a point to ask her if she wanted her whole sex life paraded in court.

While she pictured her life in Tijuana coming out, Leo pictured her with him alone on the beach and in the hotel, out of wedlock. They agreed to drop it.

The policeman tossed his notes in the trash.

Leo confided in Annee about everything. He told her he wanted to marry Rosa, she was pregnant, and Entwhistle had taken advantage of her.

Annee confided in Antonio, and he saw things differently. That Tijuana slut had put Leo behind the eight ball. That bastard Entwhistle was just another trick.

Antonio confided in Ara who couldn't decide what was true. He liked Rosa and he despised Entwhistle.

Ara confided in Hovanes who had nothing to say.

Hovanes tracked Entwhistle to his apartment and confronted him. Hovanes, not nearly as animated as Ara, calmly threatened to expose Entwhistle with the rape if he didn't agree to vote for the garbage routes for Ara and Hovanes. Hovanes had no appreciation for subtlety or for such terms as blackmail. He quickly learned that his bargaining chip with Entwhistle had no value.

"That's blackmail. I'll have you and your brother thrown in jail." Entwhistle laughed out loud. "Who are they going to believe. You Turk-fodder Armenians or me? You are going to lose everything. You want to read in the Times that you offered me $50,000 in cash to vote for garbage routes? You want an investigation?"

Checkmated, Hovanes quietly shrugged away. But business aside, there was something deeper in Hovanes' psyche and in his character, that Entwhistle did not count on.

Hovanes respected women. It came from having a loving mother and a father who adored her.

The pivotal point in Hovanes' life took place when he was a young boy. Held by a Turkish soldier, he stood and listened outside the family hut in Armenia in 1915, to other Turkish soldiers, one after another, raping his mother, before shoving a scimitar through her body.

"There is your mother," the ugly Turk pronounced, holding Hovanes by the scruff of his neck and pushing his head into the hut. His mother lay motionless on the bed, a look of horror on her face. His father lay sprawled on the floor next to the bed, covered in blood.

Entwhistle's treatment of Rosa was not lost on Hovanes.

The day after Entwhistle dismissed Hovanes, Hovanes returned. He pulled up in his car just as Entwhistle arrived home and asked Entwhistle to get in. Hovanes said he was sorry about the day before, the blackmail talk.

"Can we going for drink, I have something very good for you?" Entwhistle thought twice about the offer, then said "OK."

Hovanes, serially forged by love, hate, and steel, drove only three blocks to an alley where he crushed Entwhistle's larynx with his thumbs while choking him to death.

Fortunately for the Avakians, Entwhistle had not confided in anyone about the bribes he had taken from them, not even his father. Luckily, also, Entwhistle had buried most of the cash from the Avakians at his parent's house in Beverly Hills, where he had played as a youngster, in a steel box in a grove of trees in the back yard, where it was never to be found.

Seeing headlines of Entwhistle's murder in the LA Times, the Hollywood policeman remembered the young Mexican couple who had reported Entwhistle about the rape.

The policeman had a sketchy recollection of the girl getting a ride from Entwhistle from some garbage magnate's house. The policeman wondered if the crime was payback for Entwhistle. Because the policeman did not document the interview, as he should have, he did not report anything to the detectives assigned to the investigation of the murder. Besides, he believed the young girl and liked both her and her boyfriend.

The Times ran Entwhistle stories for weeks, until a special evening edition of the paper hit the streets on December 7, 1941, with breaking news of Pearl Harbor.

Leo had married Rosa only a couple weeks before Pearl Harbor and moved in with Rosa and Carmen. They all knew the cramped conditions would be short-lived. It was only a matter of time, shorter than they thought, before the US got into the war.

The Sunday barbecue at Ara's was deadly serious on the day the Japanese bombed Pearl Harbor. Leo said he wanted to join the military and was thinking about the Marines.

"You've got a wife; and, a baby on the way." "You don't have to go. Wait 'til they call you."

Leo waited. The baby came, a little girl, Angela. A week later, Leo enlisted, and a month later he was in training at the Marine Corps Recruit Depot in San Diego. He got additional training at Camp Pendleton and was able to see Rosa and the baby a few times before shoving off. He phoned his father and told him that Marine training was best described as 101 ways to kill someone with your belt buckle.

"We're all praying for you, Leo. Be brave, but get back."

Next stop, a place called the Solomon Islands. Marines, Navy and Seabees island-hopped, along with task forces under Nimitz and Halsey that were trying to outmaneuver the Imperial Navy to buy time to rebuild the American fleet, and once powerful enough, head for Japan. The Army was there too, right behind the Marines. Leo got to know a Navy pilot, a Pensacola class of '42 graduate who dropped out of college and enlisted before the war, Mickey McGonigle. They played catch together and got into some baseball games.

Mickey took Leo up in his SBD and gave Leo the ride of his life. Mickey told Leo about his first combat in the Solomons. He had just come over a peak, where right below, getting ready to take off, were two Japanese Jennies, both big bombers, with crews of ten men. Mickey did a barrel roll and loop to avoid ground fire, climbed into the sun, flipped over, and raced earthward to drop a single bomb between the taxiing Jennies. He was on target. Fully fueled and armed, the Jennies exploded into smithereens.

Mickey was always in competition, particularly with another pilot, Bill Weaver. The Jenny kills kept Mickey ahead in their race to deplete enemy forces. Weaver had lettered in three sports at Ohio State. Mickey, a New Yorker, had gotten a football scholarship to Randolf-Macon, a small southern college in Ashland, Virginia. He played both football and baseball and was Phi Beta Kappa en route to an aeronautical engineering degree, when in 1941, he left college, joined the Navy and applied for flight training.

Mickey got with Weaver to organize a baseball tournament. Five teams, winner take all, for a $500 pot, costing each team $100 apiece to enter. A lot of the officer participants had played college ball and Weaver's team was stacked with them, including a Pacific Coast Leaguer, Dale Ford, who could hit the ball over 450 feet. Mickey's team was notably eclectic and diverse, sporting a Mexican, a colored, and what the opposition was convinced, had to be a queer. Mickey was convinced too, but saw him only as a hell of a short stop.

Mickey democratically doled out equal shares of the $500 to his teammates after they won it all. Hardly anyone could hit off Leo, or steal off Mickey, the colored kid roamed the entire outfield side line to side line to pick off fly balls, the queer turned six double plays and relayed a strike to Mickey cutting down the only runner to round third base in the whole tournament against them. The day they won ranked as one of the happiest days of the war for them, right up there with going home, V-E and V-J days.

◦◦◦

Leo landed before dawn on a small island inhabited by Japanese soldiers and island natives. He scouted a small area of the island with Hiram Biggs, a sharp shooter from Alabama. They found a well fortified Japanese stronghold and a native village on the northern side of the island. They called in coordinates to their lieutenant and dug in to watch the fireworks. Navy shells started landing about 2:00 a.m. A couple of them looked like direct hits. The shelling went on for about thirty minutes, strobe-lighting the whole windward side of the island. About half of the Japanese military fortifications appeared knocked out.

Leo called for a second strike at modified coordinates. Between strikes, in a field below, he saw a little native girl, crying alone. An errant shell from the first barrage had hit near her village dispersing many of the villagers in all directions. Leo told Hiram to cover him.

He was going for the girl without his rifle. The shells began landing off target, one, close enough to knock both Leo and the little girl off their feet. Leo was up in an instant, running to get to her as quickly as possible.

Before he could reach her, he saw another figure also running toward the girl, but coming from the direction of the fortifications. The figure, a Japanese soldier, had a rifle in his hand. Leo thought better about getting the girl but the shells were exploding all over the place, and no one was safe anywhere on that side of the island.

Leo thought he could reach the girl ahead of the Japanese soldier, and he did, barely. He grabbed her arm and just as he did the Japanese soldier grabbed the other one. They lifted the girl up and ran away from the incoming shells.

Hiram was squinting to take out the Japanese soldier but he did not have a clear shot in the intermittent flashes of light. The Japanese soldier knew where he was going, to the safety of a hollowed out hillside, reinforced with stacked sections of cut palm trees.

After ducking inside for cover, the two fighting men looked at the girl who was still crying but apparently unscathed. The men looked at each other. The Japanese soldier had not seen any Americans and was surprised to see one as dark as Leo. *Americans didn't look like that in the movies*, he had seen in Tokyo. Leo went after him and his rifle, taking the gun away and pointing it in the soldier's face.

Leo took the girl by the hand and backed away still aiming at the soldier. Leo made his way back to Hiram with the girl and the three of them got safely back to the unit. Fighting lasted three days.

The Marines took moderate casualties and the Japanese fought to their deaths — including the one Leo spared.

When the fighting stopped, Leo returned the little girl to her village, in a happy and tearful reunion with her family.

Fighting got worse on the Marianas. In the dead of night, Leo plunged his bayonet into a seventeen year-old Japanese sentry, who was taking a pee, and twisted the knife exactly how he had been taught at MCRD. He peeled the clothes off the dead soldier, stripped down to his own skivvies, and put on the Japanese uniform. Capture in the enemy uniform meant torture and death. He worked his way along a ridge near several Japanese big gun and mortar installations. He wore a rucksack with dozens of grenades in it. His mission had been prompted when Navy ships could not zero in on several Japanese installations, located on high ground, that kept pummeling advancing troops.

A Marine Captain, David Jackson, bucking for promotion, convinced headquarters of the plan. He would send the best man he had in the dead of night to damage the installations with grenades. He chose Leo because he knew Leo had an arm like Bob Feller.

After killing the first Japanese soldier, and before reaching the summit where the installations were housed, Leo met three patrols, two Japanese soldiers in each. Wearing the Japanese helmet, uniform, and cover of night, it allowed Leo to walk up to the patrols with his index finger to his lips, signaling not to say a word, before he wielded his weapons for the kills. His kill count included seven Japanese by the time he started pulling out the grenades from the rucksack for the task at hand. He set ten grenades near the closest installation then belly-crawled to each of the remaining installations. He tied a white handkerchief knee high to the bark of the palm tree nearest each stash of grenades to help him find them on his way back. The air was moist and heavily perfumed.

He pulled a pin and let fly the first grenade. Then he threw three more grenades, pins in, in rapid succession. The next grenade, he threw pin-out and it set off the others, doing considerable damage. He threw three more, pins in, and two more pins out. The big gun was damaged and inoperable. Its crew, wounded or dead.

Leo crawled the underbrush of the jungle hillside, now being combed by numerous enemy patrols, to track down the remaining stashes of grenades. He was able to hurl all the grenades, as planned, at the other installations.

On his way back to American lines he came across two more Japanese soldiers. He thrust his bayonet into one, leaving him to stagger while stabbing the other with a knife.

When Leo got close enough to his own lines he tore off a branch from a tree, took the enemy uniform off and stuck his skivvies on the end of the tree branch. Naked, carrying the flag of truce, he ran from the Japanese held side of the island to the American side. Several rifle shots were fired at him from behind but missed. The Americans shot over his head for cover.

He briefed the captain on each detail of the mission and never spoke another word about it.

Apart from still breathing, Leo's great gift of the day was a letter from home: "Angela looks more like you every day. Yesterday she piled stuffed animals in the corner of the playpen, pulled herself up on the rail, straddled it for a second and flipped onto the hardwood floor. Luckily her padded bottom took the brunt of the landing. 'Mama, I gumped' she said."

This made Leo smile and almost laugh. He folded the letter neatly, shoved it into an envelope and tearfully prayed himself to sleep, picturing Angela and Rosa, while trying to erase any thought of the young Japanese boys he had killed.

CHAPTER X

1945

IN OCTOBER 1945, Leo was reunited with Mickey McGonigle who ran air operations on a carrier, the Yorktown, serving as a troop ship from the Gilbert Islands in the western Pacific to Hawaii. He and Mickey got stinking drunk two nights in a row in Honolulu and vowed to stay in touch when they got back to the States.

Leo was assigned to take a Matson liner from Honolulu to San Francisco for the trip home. It was filled with the wounded and other survivors who seemed to take turns playing cards and throwing up. Leo gave five dollars to a one-armed barber, named Ziggy, an Army corporal from Wilkes-Barre, Pennsylvania, who tirelessly and cheerfully cut the hair and shaved the faces of the boys coming home.

After land was sighted, the sailors, soldiers and marines who could walk and stand, moved their wheelchair and stretcher-bound comrades near the starboard rails and lined up behind them as the sleek, white pleasure cruiser moved into San Francisco Bay before turning south and finally sliding gently against a long pier in front of cheering crowds.

—⊰●⊱—

Leo had a decision to make. California or Utah. He waited to bring it up to Rosa. Their first days together focused purely on the senses. They made up for their time apart with lovemaking morning, noon and night, great meals, and hot showers. Carmen helped out before going off to El Coyote for the lunch crowd, by taking the baby for long walks to give the reunited couple time alone. Life was good for the first time in a long time. Leo expected nightmares, cold sweats and depression to follow him home. He had seen a lot of it among his fellow troops from first battle to last. But for whatever reason, none of it happened to him.

"Rosa, I'm thinking about what to do. We should go to Utah to visit my folks before I start back to work. Antonio asked me to come back in three weeks. He wants me to drive for a year or two then bring me into the office."

"I'd love to meet your family."

On November 12, 1945, the same Matson liner that brought Leo back cruised under the Golden Gate Bridge down San Francisco Bay toward Pier 19. Alcatraz was barely visible, port side, in a misty rain. Fog shrouded the east bay.

Eddy Velasco's face was cold and wet.

He looked starboard toward the city's skyline, but what he was looking at, did not register. He was thinking instead of his shipmates, the submarine attack, lethal torpedoes, deafening explosions, hellish groans, cries of agony, treading water in an oil slick, and sharks.

The ocean had been his mistress too long. He was ready to go home.

Eddy was billeted at Treasure Island half way across the Oakland Bay Bridge, waiting for the Navy to finish the paperwork for his discharge.

He went into the city alone one evening and wandered aimlessly about its streets. He watched the sun go down from high on a hill. It was windy and raw.

The chill in his bones was welcomed. It reminded him of home.

It felt good to be cold again after years in the South Pacific.

He stopped for a moment under a street lamp to have a smoke.

He was lost in thought when a young woman approached him. "Got a light, sailor?"

It was a line from a VD training film Eddy had seen. *She must be a hooker*, he thought.

She wasn't.

He lit her cigarette.

"Thanks," she said.

"Say are you going to the Fairmont?"

"Fairmont?"

"Harry James is playing."

Eddy shook his head *No* and she kept on.

Later that evening he found himself near the Fairmont Hotel. Crowds from the street were pouring into the carriage area and through the main doors. But Eddy was not in the mood for any fun. "Where are you from sailor?" asked a well-dressed man in civilian clothes, accompanied by a young lady in a red woolen coat, black fur hat and muff.

"The USS Indianapolis, Sir."

"Where's it stationed?"

"It," Eddy thought, "She sank."

"Sorry to hear that. Come on. We'll buy you a drink."

They whisked him along into the luxurious lobby of the Fairmont Hotel down a corridor and into a high-ceilinged room with mahogany bar and mirrors. It was crowded with civilians and service people alike. The three were lucky to find enough chairs to squeeze together at a table for two.

"Well, where are you from, originally?"

"Smithton, Utah."

"Oh, the Mormons. Polygamy. You don't strike me as a Mormon." Of course he didn't. Eddy was dark with huge black eyes. *Sexy eyes*, the woman thought, removing her hat and coat to expose a patterned black and white polished-cotton dress clinging to a perfect figure. She looked a lot younger to Eddy than her sophisticated attire had first suggested. Up close, even in the half light, with bluish smoke swirling about the room, it was clear she was no older than Eddy. The man had at least a decade on the two of them. To the man, Eddy looked like any number of workers (*braceros*) from his father's farm in Monterey, or the heavily accented Latino recruits from Fort Ord that he had measured for Army uniforms in the summer of 1943, when he had done his patriotic duty stateside.

"I'm Charles Wallingford and this is Miss Platt."

"How do you do. I'm Ed Velasco."

"Velasco? Spanish?"

"Somewhere back, I suppose. I have always thought of myself as Mexican."

"Your English is perfect."

"I went to school through eleventh grade in Smithton."

"Here in California, not all Mexican children go to school."

"I know," Eddy said. Correcting himself, "I mean, I figured as much."

A waiter stood over them. "What would you like," he shouted, above the din of the crowded bar.

"The lady would like a high ball, bourbon and ginger ale. I would like a vodka martini," Wallingford paused, looking at Eddy.

"I'll have what the gentleman is having."

After two rounds, Eddy was feeling it. Charles Wallingford, like others who had stayed behind, had more questions than a beat reporter. Miss Platt remained silent. Eddy looked back and forth at the two of them as if at a tennis match.

The man had kind eyes, Eddy concluded, and she had secrets behind hers. When Charles excused himself to go to the men's room, Eddy looked at her and smiled. Strains of "Kiss Me Once" and sweet trumpet notes were coming from the nearby ballroom.

Eddy offered the young lady a smoke by pulling out a pack of Chesterfields. With the same hand, he shook the package and the tips of several cigarettes shot up for the taking. He held them out to her. She politely refused, so he tugged one out for himself by the lips and lit up. He could not think of anything to say, and she, it seemed, would not talk. Finally, Eddy said, "What do you do?"

"Telephone operator."

"Oh."

Silence.

"No wonder you don't talk much."

She laughed for the first time. She quickly erased the lingering smile that followed, when she caught sight of Charles, returning.

They offered to drop Eddy back at Treasure Island but he declined. He ended up getting into a taxicab on Sacramento Street, already half full of drunken sailors when it pulled over. He waited to get back to his barracks before pulling out the crumpled napkin Miss Platt had placed in his hand under the table at the end of the evening.

"Call me," it stated, "dial '0' and ask whoever answers for Dorothy Platt."

Eddy called her the next morning. She suggested a restaurant in Chinatown on Grant Street after work. She was a different person than the night before. Animated, joking, easily manipulating chopsticks, and challenging Eddy to do the same. She chose several entrees for the two of them that they washed down with cold bottles of Chinese beer.

A single candle flickered between them in a metal, ornate cup, constructed with dragon figures, that sat in a porcelain saucer atop a wooden, black lacquered table top. Her dreamy eyes glowed in the half-light.

After eating, and once outside, wet biting cold and heavy sobering air engulfed them. "Walk me home, I have to operate early tomorrow," Dorothy said, holding up the back of her hands, like a surgeon. Eddy flashed on surgical operations in bloody infirmaries, he had seen, then laughed aloud, as much at himself, for not getting her joke, as finally getting it.

Her place was the back half of the bottom floor of a three story Victorian house on Folsom Street. She had private access, a hot plate, a small refrigerator, a sitting area and a bed divided from the sitting area by an Oriental screen. The place was small and neat with a hint of perfume. The bathroom was out a door and down a hall, shared with two other girls. Eddy and Dorothy took turns using the facilities after all the beer they had drunk.

Dorothy had come to California from Ogalala, Nebraska with her brother, Billy, in 1944. She was twenty at the time she came west; Billy, eighteen. He was stationed at the Presidio. Her mother had died when she was nine. Her father, a Presbyterian Minister never remarried. Billy had turned into a wild kid, the rebel son of a preacher. Dorothy tried to mother him.

She and Billie shared her little flat on weekends whenever Billy could get leave, before he shipped out.

Billy's glass-enclosed picture, with him in uniform, stared back at Eddy from a standing frame on the end table next to the sofa. Eddy would never ask who it was, but Dorothy, seeing Eddy looking at the photograph, volunteered. "My brother."

"Oh. Where is he now." "Killed in Okinawa."

"Killed in," was an expression that Eddy hated. "Sorry."

"Look, thanks for walking me home. I like you but I'm engaged to Charles. I thought it would be nice to get to know you while you were in town. Anyway, maybe we can see each other again before you leave."

"Sure. I'll be around for about another week. When would it be convenient for you?"

"Thursday night, after work. Do you like jazz?"

⸺⫷⫸⸺

Dorothy never got over Billy. When she got the news of his death, she went crazy for a while. She did not want to go back to Nebraska for good but went for a week to see her father.

Her supervisor at the telephone company gave her the time off. When Dorothy returned to work, she was still extremely depressed. She could not do her job. Her supervisor finally asked the manager if she could let Dorothy go. The manager, Charles Wallingford, met with Dorothy, took an interest in her, and nursed her back to the stage of mental health that she currently enjoyed. Still fragile.

⸺⫷⫸⸺

Dorothy missed work on Friday. Charles dropped by at noon to see how she was doing.

When she was not at home, Charles thought about contacting hospitals, but he didn't. Still, he came back to her apartment after work. She was there. She told him that she had taken a long walk and was thinking about the two of them. From the look on her face and the tone of her voice, Charles knew what she would say. "I don't think I can marry you."

⸺⫷⫸⸺

That same day Eddy boarded a Greyhound bus from San Francisco bound for Salt Lake City. His head was filled with coming home, memories of war, what to do for a living, and Dorothy. The night before, after several drinks at the jazz spot and going back to her apartment, he had held onto her all night. Lovemaking came tenderly for the two first-timers. It drained them momentarily of the war and what it had done to them.

But the next morning, Dorothy woke up and slipped out of bed to put clothes on. She felt guilty for what she had done. "I'm sorry, Eddy. You know I'm going to marry Charles."

She missed work that day and walked all over San Francisco.

⎯⎯⎯◈⎯⎯⎯

The gully hadn't changed. A fresh snowfall made it hush and serene. The houses looked less decrepit covered in snow.

Eddy, warm except for his feet, wore his dark navy winter wool uniform topped with a pea coat. He carried a duffle bag slung over his shoulder.

A scrunching sound marked each footstep through the dry snow. When he got to the doorstep, instead of just walking into the house as he always had, he felt strangely compelled to knock.

His mother opened the door. She looked a lot older now. Her hair was no longer streaked with greying strands, but all white.

"Mama."

"Mi hijo!"

She and Eddy shared a loving look before reaching for each other.

Eddy's mom cried on his shoulder.

All the while he patted her head, smiled and held back his own tears. It was the same drafty house. And it smelled the same. It smelled like *chorizo*, lingering from the early breakfast Eddy's mom had made for herself. She asked Eddy what she could fix for him.

"*Huevos rancheros.*" Eggs, ranch style. In their house, that meant with *chorizo*, spicy pork sausage.

"You missed Leo," she said, "he was here with his wife and baby girl."

"They're still in Los Angeles?"

"Yes. Very nice girl, Rosa, and beautiful baby, named Angela."

"Hopefully, he'll come back for another visit some time."

"Have you thought about what you are going to do?"

"I've saved some money. I think I can raise pigs. Or maybe chickens."

"And I saved the money you sent me," his mother said, "you should talk to Don Pedro."

The "Don" had crept ahead of the name Pedro Figueroa, as a term of respect, like "Sir."

⊱⟐⊰

Eddy walked into the barber shop in Smithton and took a seat in front of a big window letting in bright morning light. He looked at the day's newspaper and waited his turn.

The barber did not acknowledge him. The other customers looked at him oddly.

Avery Monson walked in and stopped dead in his tracks. "Well, I heard you were back."

Eddy stayed put and only looked at Avery's shoes and nodded.

"I'll be right with you Doctor Monson," the barber said.

Doctor, Eddy wondered. He never thought Avery was smart enough to follow in his father's footsteps.

"So Eddy, see any action?" Avery asked strutting now like a courtroom prosecutor.

Eddy nodded.

"You know, Leo was here a couple months back, sat in the same chair you are sitting in now. I asked him about fighting the Japs. You know what he said about them?"

No response from Eddy. Just a vague look still without direct eye contact with Avery.

Sneering, Avery went on, "He said the Japs were brave soldiers."

Eddy looked Avery right in the eye now. Still not willing to say a word.

"Can you believe that — the Japs — brave soldiers — well, they got it good last August in Hiroshima and Nagasaki, got what they deserved for Pearl Harbor and everything else, don't you agree?"

Eddy kept his gaze on Avery but had no words to say to him.

"You know Eddy, Leo didn't get his hair cut here."

Eddy had not thought twice about walking into the barber shop. But Avery's surly tone now reminded him that the shop had never catered to Mexicans. Eddy had changed in a lot of ways in his time away, but Smithton hadn't. The barber would have let him sit there all day and never taken him.

"No Mexicans here, Eddy. What's with you returned servicemen, anyway? America is still not an integrated society, you know. Separate but equal."

Eddy stood up quickly and Avery flinched. Then Eddy walked out.

Avery sauntered arrogantly over to the table with the magazines on it and reached for one.

⸻ «◍» ⸻

Eddy talked to Pedro Figueroa about raising pigs and was directed to the Reed family. Eddy bought three acres of land from them. The Reeds knew Eddy from high school sports. They told Eddy, as Don Pedro had, that they had lost their son Gerry in the Battle of the Bulge; and, they reminisced with Eddy over the Utah high school baseball finals of 1937 when Gerry scored what everyone thought was the winning run.

The Reeds were happy to sell Eddy a little land to get him started.

CHAPTER XI

1954

NEITHER LEO NOR Eddy fought in Korea. It was their turn to stay home.

In 1954 old Mr. Reed died and his farm went up for sale.

$18,500 for 37 acres of land. Eddy had nearly $1,200 saved and Pedro Figueroa had almost $200. They had more than enough for the down payment but neither one could convince the local bank to make them a loan. Dr. Monson offered $20,000 to Mrs. Reed after he had a private chat with Arnold Jensen, the bank president.

Martin Reed, Gerry's younger brother, talked to his mother about the offers and to an attorney in Salt Lake City near the University of Utah where Martin was attending school. The attorney drew up a land sale contract for Eddy and Pedro to buy the land over time after making a down payment of $925. The farm produced enough cash to meet the instalment payment requirements and to line a little of Pedro's and Eddy's pockets.

⸺⬥⸺

Leo sat with Ara, Hovanes and Antonio in Ara's library, with its marble floor and wooden shelves, a large Persian rug in the center, surrounded by several leather chairs, and a long ruby-colored, art deco style, mohair sofa.

"Los Angeles doubling in size post-war. The aviation industry doing good. People pouring in from all over. Television taking off. Movie industry taking a hit from TV. TV ads selling products." Ara, a shrewd businessman, was obviously going somewhere with this.

He had dreamed of getting into other businesses besides garbage, and believed that now was the time. Ara wanted to sell cars. He had his eye on three vacant lots, several miles apart, on main arteries in East Los Angeles, Whittier and El Monte.

"Leo, how would you feeling to managing car dealership."

"What are you getting at?"

"I getting at Hovanes, Antonio and me buying three dealership, you managing, and we all making money."

"I don't know anything about the car business."

"You learning. You thinking Hovanes and I knowing anything about garbage business when we starting. No. But so what. We learning it. You learning it too."

Leo had a G.I. Bill that he had considered using for college night courses in accounting but had been so busy at work, with not enough time for his family as it was, that he could never seem to get around to it. Now maybe he could take some business courses. He was a wiz with numbers.

"OK," he said. So with Ara, Hovanes and Antonio's money behind him, Leo began managing three automobile dealerships that sold new Studebaker automobiles and assorted used cars. The markups were excellent, new car volumes were strong, used car sales soared, and service was a cash cow. It was not Ford or Chevy. And that's how Leo sold the brand. Better built, more mechanically sound, and designed by Raymond Loewy himself.

The railway system Antonio, Ara and Hovanes had built with their bare hands as young men was getting paved over for the oil and car companies' benefit on taxpayer dollars.

Leo did not get directly involved in car sales, instead, kept a close eye on the books, and the people working for him. He got and kept good people, war veterans mainly, so the business took off and never looked back.

Home life pleased him most. He and Rosa lived in West Hollywood on Vista Avenue, a block off Melrose in a four bedroom house with Angela, now 13, Pedro, 9, and Elena, 8. The neighborhood was predominantly Jewish, sprinkled with Holocaust survivors, and a smattering of actors and movie people, young and old. The Figueroas were different, and definitely in the minority, but no one bothered them. Except in school, of course, where the Figueroa children met varying degrees of prejudice and taunting; but, so did short kids, fat kids, clumsy kids, braniacs and weaklings.

The Figueroa children learned to ignore and avoid bullies without becoming them. They made good grades and listened to their mother who instilled discipline in them, took them to church, saw that their schoolwork came first, all their chores got done, and no TV until everything was finished.

Rosa ruled the roost with all the love her own childhood lacked. Angela grew up with plain features wearing glasses. In the eighth grade all that changed. Her nose and cheeks were suddenly chiseled. She shot up five inches. All of her baby fat relocated in her chest and hips. Her waist measured the same as before, but optically shrunk. Awkwardness gave way to a curvy gracefulness. She got contacts.

She's a woman Rosa admitted to herself, then immediately went and warned her about boys.

When Angela entered Fairfax High School, she made friends with another Latina in the freshman class, named Isabel, who actually reminded Angela a lot of her aunt Carmen. Carmen still lived in Hollywood on Grace Street, the same place she had shared with Rosa and Leo when Angela was born.

Angela wanted to be a secretary. She would go to the dealerships with her father on the weekends and help him with his work. He paid her 35 cents an hour.

She made it through her first year of high school with honors, avoided boys, and settled into a comfortable friendship with Isabel. That summer, she went to work with her father on a daily basis and started saving money for a car. The family went to Utah for their summer vacation and stayed on their grandfather's and Uncle Eddy's farm. Uncle Eddy and Leo got up early and went fishing most days. Little Pedro and a cousin or two tagged along. There were day trips to godforsaken areas to fire off grandpa's Colt .45 and Uncle Eddy's rifles at tin cans. They even went and hiked through Zion National Park, a reddish, rocky wonderland, big, open and windy. Colors seemed brighter in Utah. It was vast and desolate, unlike LA.

Don Pedro asked Leo to come run the farm with Eddy but Leo had his life in California and could not imagine Rosa wanting to give it up. She still worked part-time with Annee on costumes, hung out with Carmen whenever she could, and spent every second, the children were at home, with them. She was a loving mother and a good wife. At 35 she had hit her stride.

On vacation in Utah she and Leo'd like to burst in the tight quarters and flimsy walls of the farmhouse. So in the evenings they would take long walks alone near the arroyo and make love, standing, sitting, lying down and leaning on each other. Rosa particularly enjoyed bending over a low lying branch of a tree with just the right spring in it to add to the rhythm of the moment. The two of them could get the bough creaking like a Stradivarius.

Leo's two-toned maroon and cream colored 1954 Studebaker President caught the eyes of the locals when he went shopping in Smithton. Once, with arms filled with grocery bags, he bumped into Avery Monson coming out of the hardware store. Leo recognized him immediately but said nothing. Avery had to do a double take.

"Leo?"

"Yes."

"It's me, Avery." "Hello, Avery." "Visiting your folks?" "Yes."

The encounter was brief and icy.

Avery had spent the war years in college at Brigham Young University and in dentistry school at the University of Southern California. He was married with two children. His office was on the main highway in front of his house which stood on land that his father once owned but split off and deeded to him. The medical doctor and dentist, father and son, were neighbors. Every Thursday afternoon, on the pretext of going to Point of the Mountain, where the Utah State Prison was located, to drill teeth and fill cavities for prisoners, Avery would go instead to a café in Santaquin run by Dolores Torres. At 2:30 p.m., Avery would park his yellow Buick with dark green interior, behind Dolores' trailer, which was behind the café. The trailer would shake mildly for about half an hour and Avery would leave $10 next to the sink on the way out.

Dolores did Avery for the money, but gobbled Eddy Velasco, for free. Eddy came calling on Dolores, typically on Friday nights. Eddy and Avery were the only two men she saw, while waiting for her husband, Alejandro Torres, to get out of prison for assault and battery. Alejandro had gotten drunk and thrown Dolores out of the pickup one night when she wouldn't stop nagging him to let her drive. The Sheriff was right behind them and saw the whole thing. Dolores wanted to drop the charges but the Sheriff had the power and the duty to bring them himself since he had witnessed the crime. Dolores could not make up her mind between her husband, Alejandro, and Eddy, a real catch for any girl in the area. Alejandro would kill Eddy if he found out about Eddy and Dolores. As far as finding out about Avery, Alejandro would most likely just take it out on Dolores. As a Mexican, with priors, Alejandro'd get life, likely, for just touching a hair on Avery's head.

Dolores told Eddy that she loved him and would divorce Alejandro when he got out. Eddy was up for it since he found Dolores wacky, beautiful and fun.

Most of all, Eddy was ready to settle down. Eddy did not know about Dolores and Avery.

⚬⟪◉⟫⚬

The Studebaker was parked in the shadow of a row of poplar trees protecting it from bright sunlight on a late summer morning in Smithton.

Birds sang and people chatted. The sweet smell of plums engulfed the Studebaker. The aroma came from a brown paper shopping bag, filled with fruit, stored in the trunk of the car for the trip home. Leo, Rosa, Angela, Pedro and Elena were all in their seats.

"Adios, que les vaya bien." "Good-bye, fairwell."

"Next year you come to California and we'll go to Disneyland." Pedro and Teresa, Eddy, Leo's brothers and sisters, and their little ones, waved to the Studebaker as it pulled away. The occupants waved back and Leo tooted the horn twice. Noisy tires spun and slipped over dirt and gravel, creating a cloud of dust.

None of Leo's Utah family ever came to Southern California. It seemed the only place they felt comfortable was the farm or the gully. Salt Lake City was too big and too busy for them. They felt out of a place among all the gringos with their light eyes, cold manners, and sandy hair.

Mexicans were not welcome in any businesses, either, followed around like shoplifters wherever they went.

"Dad, what do you know about civics?" Angela asked. "Civics?"

"I have to take it next year."

"Well, I remember a little from high school, and reading the paper."

"You read the paper every day, don't you?"

"Yeah, your Uncle Antonio used to hand it to me when he finished with it when I lived with him when I first came to California. He told me to read the whole thing because he would quiz me on it.

"Antonio told me that my dad had taught him to read when they tended sheep in the mountains of New Mexico and I think Antonio got started then and never stopped. The man is a voracious reader.

"As far as the newspaper, I never gave up the habit. For civics I can tell you who's the President, Vice-President, the Mayor, the Governor, and, government has three branches, executive, legislative and judicial. The legislature has two houses. That means bicameral. The Senate and House of Representatives. Both houses are elected directly by the people from their respective districts and states. The number of representatives depends on the state's population. The bigger the state, the more representatives, 435 in all. Each state has two Senators. The President and Vice-President are elected by an electoral college where, usually, each state gives all of its electoral votes based on the state's population to whichever candidate wins the majority of the popular vote in that state. For example, a small state might have 3 electoral votes, a big state 15. Whichever candidate gets more than half the popular vote gets all 3 or all 15 votes. Then you add up all the electoral votes from all the states and see which of the candidates has a majority of them. He wins. The President is Commander-in-Chief of the armed forces. But the legislature has to vote to declare war. State and local governments follow the same patterns with an executive, a legislative body and, of course, a judicial system of judges and courts. I don't think states employ electoral colleges on a state level. Whoever gets the most votes wins."

"Whew. Who do you think will be the next president?"

"Nixon."

"Why do you say that?"

"He's the Vice-President. I heard Ara talking about it with Antonio. Neither one of them think the Democrats have a chance."

"Have you heard about Kennedy?"

"Yes. Remember, we watched him on television speaking at the Democratic National Convention in 1956?"

"Oh, yeah."

"Some people wanted him for Vice-President but the Democrats chose Estes Kefauver instead. Do you remember any of that?"

"A little."

"Well, I guess you'll learn these things in Civics Class."

"Papa, are you a Democrat or Republican?"

"Well, I liked Ike."

"Republican then. Did you vote for him?"

"No."

"Why not?"

"I never voted for anybody."

"It's your civic duty."

"Well, I never felt I was part of anything, or party, or anything like that. What could my vote do, anyway?"

The phone rang at the office and Angela picked up.

CHAPTER XII

1959

ANGELA SPENT THE summer between her junior and senior years of high school with her grandparents, and worked with Eddy on the books for the farm. She also carried her weight in the fields, picking tomatoes and corn. She picked fruit in the orchards, and drove a pickup truck at haying time. Each night, once her head hit the pillow, she was fast asleep. She helped her grandmother, Teresa, in the kitchen and learned to make Mexican favorites like *enchiladas, tamales, pollo en mole, salsa, carne asada*, and simple *quesadillas* that she seemed to live on. She found the kitchen a novel attraction, except for doing dishes. She already knew how. Her mother, Rosa, had pushed the books with her, and skipped the cooking lessons. Elena, her younger sister, had gotten them instead.

Angela was seventeen now.

⬛

Eddy broke it off with Dolores Torres before Alejandro got out of prison. One afternoon Eddy swung by the café. No Dolores. He walked around to the trailer and saw Avery Monson's car parked behind it. Eddy guessed Dolores must have had something wrong with her teeth.

When Eddy got close to the trailer he heard grunting and moaning coming from the back of the trailer where the bed was. Eddy stepped quietly below the window, tip-toeing to look in. Dolores wore nothing but alternating rows of sunlight and shade in a tiger-stripe pattern cast by the Venetian blinds at an angle across her body. Her rhythmic movements and striping was mesmerizing. Avery's grunting and Dolores' straddle-humping provided Eddy with an audio-visual effect that would never leave him. He was done with Dolores.

In late August, like every year, the last of the plums, apricots and peaches were ready to be picked, and the majority of the migrant workers had already left. Angela worked non-stop with her cousins to bring in the fruit. Eddy had developed a preserve label, so he had a small shed with long tables where the fruit was halved and pitted to begin the process. Angela worked beside her cousin Adela on the fruit line wielding a sharp paring knife.

Early one morning Angela told Adela that her jaw was aching and it felt like teeth were trying to break through. The two of them dismissed the notion since neither one had ever heard of anyone getting teeth after childhood. The pain grew worse. Next day, after a sleepless night, and a couple hours on the fruit line, Angela felt faint. Adela took Angela to the house and told Teresa that Angela had to see the dentist. The Mexican dentist was in Salt Lake City. Teresa called him and he said that it was her wisdom teeth. She might need them out and she should go to the local dentist for it. Adela drove Angela to Avery Monson's office.

The receptionist greeted them coldly, completely unaccustomed to Mexican patients. No one from the gully had ever gone to Avery Monson. The receptionist had the girls sit down and wait.

The receptionist went through a door and returned after a moment. Another twenty minutes passed during which time high speed drilling sounds could be heard from within, before a patient came out, tapping the side of her face, trying to get some feeling back into it.

"You stay here," the receptionist warned Adela before leading Angela through the door.

"Sit here, Dr. Monson will be right with you."

She sat quietly for several minutes. The room smelled like mouth wash. Dr. Monson was in his adjoining office peering at her through a peephole he had devised. She wore a sleeveless white summer blouse, made of cotton, with lots of buttons and no collar. She also had on pedal pushers, patterned in three shades of green, and beige canvas slip-on shoes. Her head was wrapped in a yellow bandana. She had huge eyes, high cheek bones, an inviting mouth, and long straight nose.

"Angela?"

"Yes."

She looked at the man standing before her. He wore a thinlipped smile. He had tiny grey eyes. He was hunched over a bit leaning toward her with narrow shoulders and small bony hands. He was tall and thin. "Are you one of Pedro's children? Or grandchildren?"

"I'm his granddaughter, Leo's daughter."

"I see. Is your family visiting?"

"No. Just me."

He looked right through her.

"I'm going back home to Los Angeles soon. I came for the summer."

"Oh."

"Well, what brings you here?"

"My whole jaw aches, the pain is getting worse, my gums are sore, I can taste blood at the back of my mouth."

"Let's take a look."

"It's your wisdom teeth. They're impacted. You are how old?" "Seventeen."

"Well you are a very mature girl. How long have you been having your period?"

Angela was dumbfounded by the question.

"How long, sweetheart. I have to know these things."

"Since I was thirteen."

"I see."

"You are not in your period now, are you?"

"No."

"When was your last one?"

"Two weeks ago."

"Look you need to have those teeth extracted right away. I can do it over lunch. Is anyone with you."

"My cousin, Adela."

"How old is she?"

"Twenty-two."

"Good. You go back to the reception area and wait with your cousin. I'll talk to my assistant and we will get ready."

Avery Monson had a lot to do quickly. He had Adela sign for the operation and told her to come back at 3 o'clock. He would administer an anesthetic to Angela and she would be coming out of it at that time. He had his receptionist help him prepare for the operation then had her go to Provo, nearly an hour away, to pick up certain supplies, including a special clove tincture. He gave her the rest of the day off.

Adela went back to the farm and told Teresa what was happening. It was not until after the noon hour that Eddy came by the fruit shed and asked where Angela was. No sooner had Adela related the story to Eddy about Angela's wisdom teeth than Eddy jumped in his pick-up truck and headed for the highway.

Avery Monson heard a vehicle pull up. He glanced out the window and recognized Eddy's truck. He shoved Angela's bra over her bare breasts and furiously buttoned up her white blouse. The sign on the outside of the dentist office read *Closed*. Eddy banged on the door with his fist. After a moment, Avery Monson, in a white smock, opened it.

"Have a seat, I have to get back to my patient."

"What are you doing to her?"

"I had to pull her wisdom teeth. I'm almost done."

"I'm coming in."

"You can't."

"I am."

"Do you want me to call the Sheriff, Eddy? You can't barge in on an operation, it would be unsanitary."

Eddy glanced at the white smock and saw moist spots on it.

Eddy grabbed the smock and sniffed the spots. It was semen. He held onto the smock and, with one hand, backed Avery through the inner door.

"Don't be crazy, Eddy."

Angela lay, eyes-closed, in the dentist chair. Her hair cascaded over the back of the head rest of the chair. The yellow bandana rested on the floor beneath.

"What more do you need to do with her."

"I need to bring her out of it."

"You do that, right now."

"You know Eddy, operations like this can go wrong. You don't want her turned into a vegetable."

Eddy could have killed this negotiating bastard with his bare hands. "Look, Avery, make sure she comes out of this OK and I will leave you alone. I promise."

"You will?"

"Yes. You have my word. Just make sure she is all right."

"OK, I will."

Angela was groggy when she came to. She had not been raped. Avery did not want to deal with the mess of a virgin. Instead he had gotten off by rubbing his penis over her nipples.

Coming to, she was surprised, and comforted, to see Eddy. There had been something creepy about the dentist. Eddy helped her to her feet. She was a bit unsteady. But after a moment she said she was fine.

"Wait outside Angela while I take care of the bill with Dr. Monson."

"Oh, no charge. Not for you. Not for Leo's daughter."

"Can you go wait in my truck, Angela?"

"Sure, Uncle Eddy." She managed to walk. Eddy looked at Avery.

"Now Eddy, you don't want to do anything that will land you in jail," Avery said, backing away.

"Don't take another step," Eddy said, thinking Avery might reach for something to defend himself with.

"You said you only wanted the girl and you would leave me alone. You gave me your word, Eddy." Avery pleaded. Eddy stood still. He had on a flannel shirt, dungarees and Red Wing work shoes. The veins in his arms and hands visibly pulsated. His muscled forearms and broad shoulders could crush the skeletal frame of the taller man in penny loafers, grey woolen slacks and stained white smock.

"I have two questions for you, Avery. What did you do to Beatriz?"

"Beatriz? Nothing. Eddy, it was a complete accident. You know that road. I was driving too fast. That's all."

"You bragged at school that you screwed her."

"No. No. I never did. She. She. She wouldn't even let me kiss her. I was a kid. I didn't do anything to her. I mean it."

"Is that the truth?"

"Yes, Eddy. God's honest truth."

"What did you do to Angela."

"Nothing, I swear."

"Then why does your shirt smell?"

"My wife, Eddy. She and I had some extra-curricular here, earlier this morning. You know."

"Is that the truth?"

"Yes, of course."

Eddy looked at him for another moment, then left.

Avery had gotten away with things all of his life. Today was no different.

Eddy told Angela that the dentist might have spilled some medicine on her blouse or pants that needed to be rinsed out with a special soap, so if she could give him her clothes once they got home, he would have them cleaned. She thought nothing of the strange request. She held back giving him her brassiere even though it had some spots on it. She would never give him her panties. She ended up washing those items, herself, by hand.

Eddy smelled the clothes for any sign of Monson. Sure enough it was on the blouse. None on the pants. He drove back and found Monson alone, closing up. "You know I forgot to pay you."

"I mean it, Eddy. No charge."

"No, I insist. I brought my checkbook. How much is it?"

"Well OK, if you insist, make it sixty dollars. That's a good discount for all the hard work I did."

"*Hard?*" Eddy thought to himself. He leaned over the receptionist's desk and wrote the check. He handed it to Avery. When Avery took it, Eddy took both of Avery's hands in his. The dentist had small white hands. Eddy no longer had black and blue teenage hands from catching Leo's fastballs and curves, or hands that had held the Salt Lake Bee newspaper in them in the Smithton barber shop, the only time he had ever set foot in it. Eddy had farmer hands.

"You lied, Avery. You did something to that child."

"Please, Eddy. Please."

"Just tell me the truth and I will leave you alone."

Avery would not confess.

"Look Avery, I am not going to kill you, even though I should. I am just going to give you a little reminder. But if you tell anyone about me, I *will* kill you. And, if I die from anything other than old age, Avery, Leo will get you."

"What are you going to do to me?"

Eddy broke each of Avery's fingers, several at a time. Avery let out blood-curdling screams then passed out from the pain before Eddy finished. Avery would never work again. He would have seven surgeries on his hands, still leaving him in crippling pain. Avery told his family that the jack slipped and the car crushed his hands when he was changing a tire; a good Samaritan happened by and finished the job; Avery then drove himself home, not realizing how bad the injury had been. When his father looked at the hands he knew Avery was lying, and finished as a dentist.

Years later, Avery told his father what Eddy had done to him. He told his father that Eddy had a vendetta against him for Beatriz. When the father went for a rifle, Avery pleaded with him not to go after Eddy. But Dr. Monson saw himself above the law. He was going to kill Eddy and get off. His money would buy the right lawyer. Anyway, where was the crime in killing a Mexican? He drove to the Figueroa-Velasco farm where he confronted Eddy outside the farmhouse.

"You crippled my boy you son of a bitch."

Pedro, hearing the commotion and seeing the rifle in Dr. Monson's hand, went for his gun and came out pointing it at Monson. Dr. Monson pulled the trigger and blew away a piece of Eddy's arm. With light faster than sound, Dr. Monson never heard the shot that killed him. Pedro's pistol had gone off, sending a bullet behind Monson's ear, severing the medula, coming to rest, wedged in his shattered jaw. He collapsed in a heap on the ground.

When the Sheriff arrived, he saw Dr. Monson lying dead where he had fallen. Eddy had iodine all over his arm, that the Sheriff first took for blood. But the blood had been cleaned off. Eddy's shirt sleeve had been cut off and a clean tee shirt had been tied to his arm.

At the inquest the Sheriff stated:

"I received a call. Disturbance. Ah, disturbing the peace. At the Figueroa farm. I went out there. Dr. Monson was threatening to shoot Eddy Velasco. Claiming that Eddy had injured Avery's hands and it was a long running feud because Avery was driving the night of the prom, a couple years before World War II, with Beatriz Ordonez in the car, and he had an accident, and she hit her skull, and died. Now Dr. Monson claimed that Eddy always had it in for Avery. I since talked to Avery and asked him if Eddy broke his hands and he said 'No.' But anyway, Dr. Monson was convinced Eddy had crippled Avery. When I showed up I pulled out my Colt .45 from my glove compartment. The one I always carry. Anyway, I saw Dr. Monson unload his rifle on Eddy and saw a piece of Eddy's arm get blowed off. I told Dr. Monson to drop the weapon, but he pointed it right at me. Told me to stay out of it. He then aimed at Eddy and was about to finish him. So I shot Dr. Monson. I was only trying to wing him. I aimed for his arm but shot a little high. So that's it. I killed him trying to prevent a crime."

And that was it.

Moreover, Eddy never told Leo what had happened to Angela. Eddy thought Leo would find crippling Avery too mild a punishment and Leo would only end up at the end of a rope dangling in a steady breeze at Point of the Mountain–Utah State Prison.

CHAPTER XIII

1960

DON PEDRO AND Leo wanted Angela to go to college. Rosa was not convinced Angela needed a degree to be a secretary for her father. Angela at first sided with her mother. Angela wanted to start making a living. But in the end she listened to her Papa but mostly to her *Abuelito* (little grandfather) who told her about a night in a saloon in Socorro, New Mexico and the Shakespearian actor whose actions defied a whole town and whose words off-stage had always stayed with him.

She applied to the University of San Francisco, a Jesuit school, got in, and started classes in September 1960.

The campaign for the presidency was in full swing. There had never been a Catholic president, and John Kennedy was running. He and Richard Nixon were poised to debate.

After the first debate Angela walked precincts for Kennedy to get out the vote in San Francisco. Her first language made her an asset among minority voters in the Mission District.

What she found upset her. None of the Latinos she came across had ever voted. Many believed like her father had. Their vote would not make a difference, they did not really belong in the political process. They were resigned to menial labor and hard lives. They did not see any light at the end of the tunnel. They were the working poor.

They had no faith in politicians. They saw themselves like society did. On the bottom rung. And they knew, the way they were treated, they would stay there. What's the use?

Quietly, persistently and slowly, Angela took steps to turn these US citizens by birth into registered voters. Birth certificates, baptismal certificates, hand holding to the post office to fill out the necessary forms. Still, in the end, only a very small number of Latinos registered and voted.

On November 8th, California went to its native son, Richard Nixon. But Kennedy squeaked by in the general election with votes from the east, the south and Texas, which his vice-presidential running mate, Lyndon Johnson, had delivered.

On the registration drive, Angela had worked almost exclusively with a boy named Robby Liebowitz. As non-natives of San Francisco, they got put together just for being college students from LA. Their battle had been uphill and their efforts had done very little for voter turnout. Robby was a freshman at UC Berkeley.

After the election, Robby and Angela stayed friends and kept in touch over political events in the Bay Area. They'd occasionally attend one of them together, or spend a Sunday afternoon taking in sights, but never formally dated. Angela did not think of Robby in those terms. Robby, on the other hand, had a deep crush on Angela.

⋙⟨◉⟩⋘

Angela missed her family in Los Angeles, coming home only a few times during the school year, for Thanksgiving, Christmas and Easter.

After her first year of college she spent half the summer in Los Angeles, the other half in Utah. Her grandparents, Pedro and Teresa were sixty and fifty-seven, but not slowing down a bit. When she went to Utah, Eddy asked her about San Francisco, and told her he had spent a couple weeks there after the war. Eddy wondered to himself, as he occasionally would, if Dorothy Platt and Charles Wallingford were happy together.

Angela's family caught up to her in Utah for the first two weeks in August. Elena, Angela's sister, had been helping Rosa on costumes for *Irma La Douce* and wanted to get a job, like her mother, with the studios. Pedro had finished his first year of high school. He had no clue what he wanted to do. But for a summer job, he chose Uncle Antonio's garbage routes over his father's car dealerships and the rigid supervision he was sure to get there.

Pedro got excellent grades in high school. He made the freshman basketball and baseball teams. He also went to a track meet when his PE coach recruited him, pleading for bodies one weekend. Pedro medaled in the 100 yard dash, the pole vault and the shot put. He attributed his winning to the scarcity of opponents at sectionals and to the fact that only one other contestant at his level appeared to have spent more than ten minutes learning to pole vault.

CHAPTER XIV

1963

IN 1963, TELEVISION news showed footage of Buddhist monks wrapped in orange garbs sitting on the ground with their hands held out as if in meditation seconds before swirling flames engulfed them in a place called South Vietnam.

The word the newscasters used was self-immolation. It was suicidal. Similar, more frequent and equally nauseating news footage, became ordinary fare for nightly news.

Within weeks, that country's leader, Diem, was assassinated. Angela learned from TV news that the US was helping South Vietnam defend against communist infiltration from North Vietnam. American military advisors had been sent to Vietnam under Kennedy. The French had been there for twenty years before but had pulled out in 1954. After Korea, Eisenhower and his advisors were against involving the US in distant and costly conflicts, and did not want to feed America's military-industrial complex.

On a Friday morning, a month after Angela first heard of the assassination in South Vietnam, she was walking through the history wing of the liberal arts building at the University of San Francisco on her way to class, when she saw a fellow student, John Schaeffer come running down the hall in her direction. Without slowing down, he blurted out, "They shot Kennedy." She turned to ask details but he was strides away. She went to her next class which was abuzz with the news. Her teacher, Melvin Corliss announced that Kennedy had been shot in Dallas, Texas, where he was campaigning for a senator, named Ralph Yarborough. Kennedy was in a motorcade, and he and the governor of Texas, John Connally, had been shot. Connally had yelled out that they were going to kill us all. But both Jackie Kennedy and Mrs. Connally, riding with their husbands, were unharmed. The President and the Governor had been taken immediately to a hospital named Parkland Memorial.

The intercom in the classroom crackled and it was the school's dean announcing that he was going to provide a live-feed of the news over the intercom for everyone to listen to. Over the next minutes the garbled sound of Walter Cronkite's voice provided the same repeated details, then he said, at 1:00 p.m. Central Standard Time President Kennedy was pronounced dead. Angela had sat in stunned-disbelief as the news unfolded.

Upon word that the President was dead, the class collectively gasped. Hearing other girls in class burst into heavy sobs it brought tears to her eyes. The boys squirmed in their seats, a few pounded their fists on desktops, and shook their heads, but no tears. The whole class waited for direction. The school's dean came on again and announced cancellation of all afternoon classes.

The mood outside was eerie. The dewy smell of eucalyptus filled the morning air as Angela walked across campus, getting caught up and swept away by a crowd that ushered her into the school's large chapel.

Inside, dank air gave way to a mild aroma of burning candles. She walked through the vestibule to a side aisle, made her way halfway up to the altar, genuflected, entered a pew, lowered the padded kneeler, and knelt down.

It was deathly quiet. She looked up at the vaulted ceiling then toward the altar and the many carved statues surrounding it. She took in much of the church including the stations of the cross lining the walls on both sides. She closed her eyes and prayed for a long time. Opening her eyes she focused on a nearby painting of Our Lady of Perpetual Help, only to find its dark blue colors, disproportionate figures, and severe angles disturbing.

She looked beyond the altar to the round stained-glass window behind it. The colors of the window were growing duller and the church was getting darker. She blessed herself, making the sign of the cross, slid out of the pew and genuflected. Before leaving the church, she got in a line, waited, and lit a candle.

She walked back to her dorm in a heavy mist under darkening skies. A mild breeze magnified the autumn chill and a few raindrops began to fall. She held her books, covered in oil cloth, above her head. By the time she reached her dorm she was wet, shivering and cold.

Inside, a television blared news to a crowd of students camped in front of it. Black and white images from Parkland Memorial Hospital were showing. The spokesman for the hospital stood behind numerous microphones. He had dark hair, horned-rim glasses, and was wearing a medium dark suit with thin lapels and a dark narrow tie. He held his right hand up, slightly in front, above and away from his head, and pointed back at his forehead with his index finger. His hand was in the shape of a pistol. He announced that the president had died from a fatal gunshot wound to the head.

Pictures of Air Force One, the President's plane were shown next. Walter Cronkite announced that Lyndon Johnson had been sworn in as the 36th President of the United States while the plane was still on the tarmac; and, a shooting suspect was captured, Lee Harvey Oswald. A still photo of the swearing-in was shown. More than a dozen people could be seen in the wide angle shot looking toward a woman with her back to the camera and an obvious bible in her hand. Lyndon Johnson, Jackie Kennedy, and Lady Bird Johnson were crowded together, with grim faces. Johnson's right hand was held up; his left, floated in air above the bible.

Yet another news flash reporting that the alleged assassin, Oswald, an employee of the Texas Book Depository from which shots were fired, and from which a mail-order Mannlicher-Carcano rifle was retrieved from the sixth floor, was captured in a movie house where he had tried to hide. He had also reportedly shot and killed a Dallas policeman, J. D. Tippet.

Angela could not ignore the coincidence that Johnson, a Texan, was now President, because of events that unfolded in his home state. The students listened attentively to one news bulletin after the next. The line for the public phone in the dorm stretched down one hall and into another. Students waited politely. Angela eventually got in line and got through to her parents in Los Angeles. They were deeply saddened by all of the events and asked her if she wanted to come home early since she would be out of school in a few days anyway for the Thanksgiving holiday. She wanted to go home, but had a test, she said, she had to stay for. When she hung up with her parents, the phone rang.

"All Saints Dorm," she answered. "May I speak with Angela Figueroa?"

"This is she." She recognized the voice even as she spoke. "Robby?"

"Yes. Isn't this terrible?"

"Yes."

"I want to see you."

"OK."

"What do think about all of this?"

"I don't know what to say. It's awful."

"Tomorrow," he said, "meet me at Golden Gate Park where they rent skates."

It had been a staging area for them for getting out the vote and Angela was familiar with it. "Sure. What time?"

"8 a.m.?"

"OK."

The idea of seeing Robby the next morning was comforting.

⎯⎯⎯◉⎯⎯⎯

Robby was brimming with news.

"I spent time with a poli-sci professor last night. He said Kennedy and his brother, Bobby, made enemies with the wrong people in the South. Southerners hate the Kennedys. Like they hate Blacks and Jews. They don't go for eastern intellectuals or Catholics, either. They are against integration. The Kennedys sent the National Guard in and upset the most powerful politicians in the South. In 1961, Kennedy was on his way out, according to conservatives, after the Bay of Pigs, when he wouldn't OK air cover or send in US military to Cuba, but all that changed with Kennedy's polls late last year after the Cuban missile crisis, that made him a shoe-in for reelection. And, the Republicans don't have anyone to run against him. The professor said that the Kennedys were annoyed with Johnson over the Bobby Baker scandal and there had been speculation about dumping Johnson from the Democratic ticket next year."

"What are you saying?"

"I'm saying this could have been a power play."

"I couldn't help but consider the coincidences, given where it happened, in Johnson's back yard. But Robby, come on. Who would believe it? Besides, it only takes one crackpot like Oswald to do what he did."

"Oswald went to Russia after his stint in the Marines and has a Russian wife."

"What does that prove?"

"I don't know."

"Do you think he was put up to this?"

"I don't know, but people kill for a reason," he paused, "or, they're nuts."

"Do you think this has anything to do with the assassination of Diem in Vietnam?"

"I don't know."

"I can't wait to hear what Oswald has to say."

Sunday, November 24, 1963, in Washington D.C. was a beautiful, crisp, fall day, awash in bright sunlight.

Unknown to both sets of their parents, Angela and Robby stood on a sidewalk on Pennsylvania Avenue across from the Treasury Building awaiting a riderless horse with saddle turned round, a flagdraped casket on a cart drawn by horses, uniformed personnel from every branch of the military, including Special Forces and Navy Seals carrying flags, surviving Kennedy family members, the new President, his wife, and other dignitaries riding in black limousines. Before the cortege first appeared to their right, Angela and Robby listened to a transistor radio, held by a man behind them, broadcasting in great detail about the scheduled events of the day. Then from the transistor radio came an announcement of the interruption of programming for breaking news from Dallas.

Bulletins had become common place over the last few days. Many coming out of Dallas. "All news services report that Lee Harvey Oswald was shot to death on national television under heavy guard and in the custody of the Dallas police during his planned transfer from the city jail in that building's underground parking garage."

The man with the radio yelled out, "They shot Oswald, he's dead!" Isolated cheers went up. Angela thought cheering was a strange reaction to the news. The news of Oswald's killing dispersed rapidly along Pennsylvania Avenue to thousands of spectators.

Once the cortege passed by, Angela and Robby felt like salmon, making their way against the surge of the crowd. They did not follow the cortege to the Capitol or stand in line outside the rotunda to walk past Kennedy's casket but saw that scene repeated on television at the airport bar.

News was on all three networks, CBS, NBC and ABC, round the clock. The ineptness of the Dallas police with Oswald seemed to take momentary heat off the Secret Service for the lack of protection it gave Kennedy. Oswald's death at the hands of Jack Ruby, a person, reportedly distraught at the killing of his President, provided yet another unexpected twist to the collective American psyche.

Angela slept with Robby's arm around her the whole flight back to San Francisco. He stayed awake, to soak in her presence and try to make sense of a crazy world. He listened to her breathe and held her hand.

<hr>

Angela told her parents about the spur-of-the-moment trip to the nation's capital. Rosa first asked her why she took off without letting her parents know. Once Angela got by that issue, Rosa asked her to tell them all about her trip. Down deep, Rosa and Leo cared more about finding out about Robby Liebowitz than DC.

"Just a friend," she said. Adeptly changing the subject, she went on, "Do you know that public restrooms say 'White Women' – 'Colored Women' – 'White Men' – 'Colored Men' on them in Washington, D.C. and Virginia, and a restroom attendant told me not to come in, and go instead, to the Colored Women's restroom?"

"Different restrooms?" Rosa said.

"Mama, that's how people are. I thought the concept of 'separate but equal' was dead. In 1896, the Supreme Court ruled in a case called

Plessy v. Ferguson that Negroes were not denied any rights under the constitution so long as they had access to public facilities and systems separate yet equal to Whites'."

"Separate. Equal. Isn't that just a way to put down minorities?"

"That's just it. You hit the nail on the head. It took the Supreme Court nearly eighty years to get it right. In 1954, the Supreme Court struck down 'separate but equal' in a case called *Brown v. Board of Education* concluding that the concept of 'separate but equal' was inherently unequal. The *Brown* case was patterned after an earlier case in California brought by Mexican kids to go to school with White kids. Education was not the same in this country for everyone. After the *Brown* case, schools had to integrate. I thought that meant that everything had to integrate, including toilets. But I guess not."

"Did you study law at the university?" Rosa asked.

"No. We learned landmark legal cases, like *Plessy* and *Brown*, in American History class."

"Angie, you are talking about the same lesson I learned when I was just a boy. Your grandfather slapped me up one side of the head and told me never to think that the Whites were better than me."

"Good old *Abuelito* Pedro."

"Well, I'm glad the two of you have learned your lessons," Rosa said, "but, unfortunately, the world is far behind you, believe me."

"I know, Mama."

"But that's why you are in college. To make the world a better place. Now are we going to meet him?" Rosa returned to point.

"Who?" Angela said coyly.

Rosa only needed to roll her eyes for the answer.

"Actually, his parents live close by, in those apartments near the La Brea Tar Pits. He asked me to a movie tomorrow night."

"Is he picking you up?"

"Yes."

"What time?"

"Seven."

"Tell him to come at six for enchiladas."

"That would be nice," Angela said, forcing a smile, and envisioning a most awkward meal.

Later that same evening, Leo and Rosa were reading in bed. He was thumbing through the current issue of "Field & Stream" magazine; she had a book, she was just starting, called "To Kill A Mockingbird."

"Why didn't you tell her to forget the movie with that kid? She is only here for a few days. She should be spending her time with us."

"Leo. She's a good kid. Practically a grown woman. So she likes a boy? So what?"

"He sounds like a political activist to me."

"You don't even know him."

"Well what are they doing, going off to Washington, D.C., on the spur of the moment?"

"They're young. History majors. They want to see history in the making."

"Traveling together. Where the hell did they sleep?"

"On the plane."

Leo was relieved by Rosa's made-up answer which she assumed was right.

"Isn't she coming to work for me?"

"Yes."

"So why does she need to do these kinds of things?"

"I don't know, Leo. Remember, you were a part of history — the war."

"I'm a man."

"Leo, I can't believe I'm hearing this from you. You wanted her to go to college. This is what you get."

"Look, when you and I met the country was getting ready for war. These kids have it too easy. Hopping on a plane. How can they afford such things? I would have loved to have skipped the war, settled into a job, and raised a family. She should take her time. Finish school. Start working."

"Now you sound like she is going to start raising a family. Calm down, Leo."

"Well, she doesn't need to date some kid whose parents would go ape if they found out their precious son was dating a Mexican."

"Come on, Leo. You don't know that."

"They're Jews. They marry their own kind. And the boys always listen to their mothers. And the mothers always find fault with the girlfriends."

"The Jews don't have a monopoly on that scenario."

"Every Jew I know is like that."

"Every one you know is like that. But I know a lot of people from the studio, Jews, who are not like that. Not anymore. There are plenty of mixed marriages. Times are changing."

"She's too young to even think about marriage."

"Who said anything about marriage? From what she had to say, this boy is not even a boyfriend."

"What does his father do?"

"I don't know."

"OK. I give. I'm tired. Want me to put the lights out?"

"Not yet."

"Is that a good book?"

"So far," she said, slipping a book mark into it and setting it on the night stand. "Come here you sexual activist before I report you to the House Committee On Multiple Orgasms." She knew Leo would cringe from such talk.

And he did. *"Por favor, Rosa."*

Rosa, Angela and Elena cleaned the house and prepared the enchiladas. They fried tortilla chips, cut into triangles, and salted them to serve with guacamole. Elena had sliced avocados in half, removed the large pit from each one and spooned out the yellow and green pulp from the shells, then crushed the pulp in a bowl with a fork, while adding chopped onions and tomatoes, lemon juice and salt, and mixing it all together. She dragged her finger through the bright green mush she had concocted and collected a dollop to bring to her lips to taste. *"Muy sabroso,"* "Very tasty," she said.

Robby had never had guacamole. He loved it. He also loved the enchiladas.

Leo forced himself to provide terse tidbits of conversation to the boy. He could not find anything about the boy he liked. Nor anything he disliked, either. Rosa kept the conversation going. It centered mostly on Kennedy. Angela had forewarned Robby not to go off on his theory about a power play, so he held his tongue.

Robby asked Leo about the war. "I served with a bunch of Marines in the South Pacific and saw some combat." No one followed up on his reply, and Leo was more than content to leave it at that.

Robby told them that his father had a shoe repair shop on Pico. His mother gave piano lessons and he played piano, violin and drums, but was not in the UC Berkeley marching band. He had an older sister, Deborah, who taught third grade and was not married. She lived at home with the parents. His parents were sent out of Poland to England the spring that Hitler completed his invasion of Czechoslovakia. 1939. Leo was reminded of the day Hitler invaded Poland; it was Leo's first workday in Los Angeles; but he was not about to share old times with this kid. Leo was soon sorry that he hadn't shared them when he learned that Robby's grandparents eventually died in concentration camps.

Angela and Robby saw "The Train" with Burt Lancaster. They neither held hands nor kissed good night. Angela thought it strange that Robby would simply walk her to the steps and say good night, without trying to kiss her. But facing Robby on the front stoop she could not see what he could, a curtain moving in the window behind her. He asked her to thank her parents again for dinner.

⟫⟪⟩⟫⟪

The next movie they saw was a few weeks later in San Francisco. It was "Tom Jones." Robby slipped his hand into hers during the movie and pecked her on the cheek when he brought her back to the dorm.

She wondered how far Robby wanted to go, particularly after seeing Albert Finney romping about, and thought it best to discourage Robby, when he called again. She wanted to remain friends. She had no desire to prime the pump of her womanly desires. Instinctively, she felt that she would react no differently than other girls in the dorms, including a few that she knew were letting their boyfriends pet them. She wanted to go to the altar someday, fully intact. And besides, she did not feel she could ever get serious with Robby. He was not Catholic.

Angela found excuses to avoid going out with Robby. He soon got the message. Still each invited the other to graduation ceremonies and dinner afterwards. Angela graduated in late May and Robby attended the ceremony. Angela apologized that she would not be in the Bay Area for his graduation. He asked if he could call her when he visited his parents in LA during the summer and she said that she did not think it was a good idea.

For Angela, the only negative about Robby was his religion. She had had any number of dates during college. Jocks and hunks, mainly, brash enough to ask her out. None of them had kept her attention. Not like Robby had. He was smarter and more sensitive than anyone she knew. Except her father. She began wrestling with the notion of religion and questioned how well it thrived on the fear of hell. Still she was glad to have landed by chance into the one true one.

CHAPTER XV

1964

ROBBY RETURNED TO Berkeley for a Masters in Education. He planned to teach high school. Angela went to work for her father. Elena got a job at the studio with her mother. Pedro graduated from high school the same year that Angela graduated from college. He started in September at the University of San Diego. The freshman class was much smaller than he had expected, less than two thousand. The school was divided into a men's and women's college. The men's, was run by priests; the women's, by nuns.

Partying and fraternities monopolized the social side of school life. There was no football team. But the basketball program was on the rise. The school had hired Phil Woolpert to coach. He had put USF on the map with two national championships in 1956 and 1957. It did not hurt to have Bill Russell on those teams. Woolpert's discipline, defensive and offensive schemes were second to none. But talent at USD ran thinner than at big schools, particularly UCLA, which had acquired Lew Alcindor of Power Memorial. The players that Woolpert brought in from inner-cities, like Washington, D.C., Los Angeles and New York City, called themselves, "Brothers."

Pedro got a job in the school cafeteria washing dishes. He needed it if he wanted spending money, his father had told him. He made friends with some commuter students who drove each day from Tijuana. The school was ninety-some-per-cent White. Pedro was used to the odds. He avoided the fraternity thing, studied hard, and got straight A-s.

The school's basketball team did reasonably well, including upset victories over San Diego State, Long Beach State and Loyola of Los Angeles. But the school was neither the size, nor was the team, the caliber, to get an NCAA playoff invitation.

Pedro spent a lot of time at the gym in pick-up basketball games and playing volleyball. Phil Woolpert saw him there and asked him why he didn't try out for the team. "Come round in the Spring, give it a try."

Pedro had played basketball in high school. But Pedro did not want to dedicate himself to sport. He liked the extra time he had for studies, and a girl he had met and fallen head over heels for, Janine Dugan.

———◄◖▶———

In August 1965, news sources reported that the North Vietnamese had attacked US ships in the Gulf of Tonkin next to North Vietnam. President Johnson asked Congress for plenary powers. Brief hearings in Congress led Secretary of Defense Robert McNamara to describe the attacks as unprovoked.

Congress gave Johnson full power to proceed. Johnson was given the authority to conduct military operations in Southeast Asia without the benefit of a declaration of war. He could take all necessary steps, including the use of armed force, to assist any member or protocol state of the Southeast Asia Collective Defense Treaty, which included South Vietnam, in response to a request for assistance in defense of its freedom. Johnson used Congress' resolution to justify escalated involvement in Indochina.

Leo was happy that Pedro was in school, far removed from Vietnam, or what might happen there. Pedro returned to San Diego for his sophomore year.

He could not wait to see Janine. They had been apart the whole summer. She had returned home to Hawaii. Her father had married a Hawaiian girl just after the war. He had had no desire to go back to Rapid City, South Dakota after serving in the Navy.

Janine was the third of five children. Four girls and a boy. She was an English major. That summer, back home, she lost her virginity to the most popular boy in high school, Tubo Tavares. She was the fifth girl Tubo had had sex with that summer and the number only increased. He was handsome, wild, a big drinker, and one of the best surfers on the island. He thought Janine had a great body. And that's all he thought about her.

Janine would not come to the phone in her dorm, or to the door when Pedro called. She avoided him completely. One evening he got a friend of his to let him into the kitchen at the Women's College. He stood at the big butler's window where the girls would bring back their dirty dinner trays. Janine was shocked to see him standing there. "Pedro, please. Just leave me alone."

"What is it? What happened?"

"Nothing. I met someone else. I'm sorry."

Not much of an explanation amid the clatter of trays, the clank of stainless steel flatware, and the groaning of the conveyor belt carrying plastic containers stacked with dirty dishes through the dish washer.

"Well, can't we discuss it?"

"There's nothing to say."

"Please."

"All right."

"Friday night, seven thirty, right after work, I'll see you at the front of the dorm."

"OK."

Janine made up some story about someone she was going with in Hawaii.

"Look, we can still go out as friends," Pedro said.

"No. It can't work like that."

And that was it. Until one evening when USD was playing San Diego State in basketball at the USD gym. Pedro sat two rows below Janine. He did not see her until he got up to stretch at halftime. "Janine, how are you?"

"Fine."

"Come on, I'll buy you a Coke."

"OK."

They got to talking. She did not like lying to him. In her eyes, he was the opposite of Tubo. Steady, reliable, good. And she knew he loved her. She did not know how to get rid of him and wondered if she should. Given her Catholic upbringing she considered herself extremely damaged goods. She decided to tell him the truth to get rid of him for his own good. When she told him, it was, of course, a body blow. His heart liked to stop, he got nauseous and weak-kneed. It was staggering information to a nineteen year old kid, attending a religious institution, about the girl of his dreams.

He looked at her. She was relieved in a strange way. Confession is good for the soul. But his expression scared her. They stood looking at each other for a moment. She thought he might hit her. He had no such intention. He tried to gather himself. His angry look morphed into stunned. He told her it didn't matter to him what she had done unless she was going back to the guy. She knew she wouldn't but she said she didn't know. After a short period of more silence, she said, "Are you going in for the second half of the game?"

"No."

"Neither am I. Can we walk together back to the Women's College?"

"I drove," Pedro said, "but I'll drop you off."

"Thanks."

For the first time they sat in a car together and had nothing to say. And for the first time he let her let herself out of the car and walk alone to the door of the dorm. Neither one of them slept that night.

—— ◆ ——

The university had a luau at the pool, next to the gym. Pedro worked the luau for the men's cafeteria which catered the food. Janine saw him. She came up to him and asked him if she could talk to him when he got off. He said OK.

"Pedro, I know you won't believe this, but I love you." Her dark eyes were pleading with him. Her flawless skin glistened under the light from a Tiki torch. Her auburn hair was pulled back tight, crowned with white hibiscus. The mouth was barely open and the neck above the collarbone wore a strand of white puka shells. Her beautiful figure was shown off by a tightly wrapped, lemon-colored sarong. She was barefoot. More pooka shells around her right ankle. Pedro wanted her, but his pride got in the way. *This is how she must have looked to her Hawaiian lover*, he thought, *only virginal then. Gee, I'd like to chuck her into a volcano.* Such thoughts only pushed him away from her.

"I don't know, Janine," he said. Not the response she was hoping for.

"I'm sorry I told you," she said, rejected more than angry. She turned quickly and walked away. After three steps, she turned back. "No, Pedro. I'm not sorry I told you. But I am sorry that you don't believe me." She turned again and he watched her walk away.

He went to his dorm room, showered and changed. He went back to the luau to look for Janine. He saw her dancing with Shane Bellows, a senior, and President of Alpha Delta Theta fraternity. He watched them from the shadows. The two of them stayed together for several songs. *Gloria, You've Lost That Lovin' Feeling, Louie, Louie, Leader of the Pack,* and *Angel Baby.* Then the band took a break. She walked toward the ladies room. When she came out, Pedro was standing near the exit.

They looked at each other. She walked up to him. "I don't know, Janine. I love you. But I don't trust you."

"Pedro, life is not a guarantee. You don't know what might happen. I had a crush on this boy and so did a lot of other girls. I don't know if I had a crush on him because I did or because they did. It's done. I can't change things. I shouldn't have told you. But I think I told you because I love you and I trust you."

"I'll think about it. Things don't happen the way you expect."

"Have you ever lost anyone close to you?"

"No."

"My younger brother was killed when he was thirteen. A hit and run. Everything seemed so much in place until then. But after that, my whole family went berserk. Each of us in our own way. That is no excuse for what I did, I know. But Pedro, you can't expect me to do what's right all the time. Look around. Hardly anyone does."

"I don't know..."

"Pedro, what *do* you know?"

"I love you, but..."

"But what?"

"I guess I wanted to be the only one for you."

"When I went home last summer I would have bet that you would be. But it didn't happen that way."

———⊙———

The following week, they went to see "Dr. Zhivago" at the Loma Theater in the '54 Studebaker President, now a relic, handed down from father to daughter, sister to brother, in the Figueroa family.

Janine squirmed during the rape and violence scenes and wept at the end.

Leaving the theater, she cried again, walking all through the parking lot, back to the Studebaker. They got in. Pedro, for lack of anything else, slipped off his tie and gave it to her to wipe the tears. She wiped them, and to Pedro's surprise, blew her nose into the tie. "Look, I ruined it," she said, wrapping it up. They both looked at it, incredulous for an instant, then burst simultaneously into laughter. Ruined indeed. He took it from her and went to toss it out the window but the window was still rolled up. "Ow," he said, midst the hard knocking sound from bashing his knuckles against the window. They both looked at each other and laughed even harder. "Let's go to the beach," she said.

He drove to the cove in La Jolla and they got out. It was cold. They walked south of the cove to the sound of breaking water. The foam was luminescent under a half moon. The air was thick with the smell of stranded sea weed and kelp at low tide. They came to a wooden kiosk. It was open air, four posted, with a roof over it. It stood atop a short cliff above the crashing surf and it was painted dark green. "I'm cold," she said, leaning into him under the roof of the kiosk. They hugged for a moment then kissed for a time. "We better get back. I have curfew," she said. He drove back holding both her hands in his right while slinging the steering wheel with his left. He felt like a spastic Steve McQueen. They parked outside the entrance to the college and kissed some more before he walked her to the door.

Their relationship deepened over time. They talked to each other several nights a week and went out weekends.

Sometimes, Pedro would go home for the weekend. He got a call from a friend of his from high school, Joe D'Amico, asking Pedro if he wanted to go to high school homecoming.

At the football game, Pedro and Joe ran into two former classmates, Bill Smith and Tom Devaney, wearing Army uniforms. They had been to Vietnam, were home for a few weeks, and had re-upped for second tours. Joe asked them about Vietnam and they told stories about fighting, going to prostitutes, and a Southern boy in their platoon getting drunk, going nuts, and blowing heads off gooks in downtown Saigon. Pedro had never heard that word before.

Bill and Tom had seen limited combat but had killed members of the NLF (National Liberation Front). They asked if Joe and Pedro were going to join up after college. Joe said, "Hell, no." Pedro told them he hadn't thought about it. "If you don't join, you'll get drafted," they said, laughing.

Then Bill Smith asked if anyone had heard about Warren Decker, a former classmate of theirs. No one had. Bill Smith told them that only last week Warren was on a med-evac mission near Da Nang when his chopper was hit. Warren got blown to bits.

CHAPTER XVI

1966

"IS ANGELA THERE?"

"Yes. Just a moment?"

"Hello."

"Angela?"

The voice was vaguely familiar.

"Yes?"

"This is Robby."

"Oh, Robby. How have you been?"

"I'm fine. But I've been drafted."

"Sorry to hear that. Where are you?"

"In town."

"Do you want to have coffee?"

"You read my mind."

"It didn't take much."

They met at the Formosa Café on Santa Monica Boulevard. He stood up when she arrived. She gave him a hug and kiss. "You look great," she said.

"So do you."

"Tell me, Robby. What have you been doing?"

"I started teaching at a high school in Mountain View last January. History. I got my draft notice and notice to appear for physical. I took my physical yesterday here in Los Angeles. 'Take your paperwork to the next station, follow the green line. Turn your head. Cough.' It lasted all day.

They took my blood pressure. The needle wouldn't move and the apparatus measured zero. They wrote down 110 over 70. I tried to flunk the hearing test but they said I passed it. Some guy dragged a nurse into the men's room and pulled a Baby Ruth candy bar, he had previously tossed into a toilet, out, and ate it. He still failed to convince the shrink he was unfit for service."

"Yuck. What are you going to do?"

"Go."

"What about conscientious objector status?"

"I don't believe in war. I think it's wrong. But I think I have a duty to the country and to the rest of the guys who are serving."

"So if you go in, when would you leave?"

"I'm probably not in for a few months. I am going to finish the semester teaching, I imagine."

"So how long are you in town?"

"Tonight and tomorrow."

"Oh."

"What's up with you?"

"Doing books and manning a phone for my dad's dealerships. I can get you a great deal on a Volkswagen."

"No more Studebakers, huh?"

"Nope."

"You like it."

"Well enough."

"Did you ever think of going back to school?"

"Not really."

"Dare I ask, got a boyfriend?"

"No. I am dating though. He thinks it's getting real serious."

"I suppose you have a date with him for tomorrow night."

"No. He'll ring me up some time tomorrow and say let's go somewhere. But no."

Robby weighed his chances. While he weighed them, Angela made it easy for him. "Are you asking?"

"Yes."

"OK."

"What would you like to do, Angela?"

"I would like to meet about three o'clock, go to an impressionist exhibit at LACMA, that's the Los Angeles County Museum of Art, have a falafel on Fairfax at 'Mi and Mi's' or maybe go to Canter's Deli, and then go to Molly Malone's afterward to listen to Irish folk music and drink Guinness beer."

"Could you be a little more specific?" They laughed.

"Didn't we do stuff like that in San Francisco after a long day of getting out the vote?"

"Yes, we did. But I don't think you can really say we got out the vote."

"No. Not really."

They talked for a while about anything they could think of, then said good night.

Angela's head hit the pillow thinking she'd missed Robby. She worried about him going to Vietnam.

⸺⊸◉⊷⸺

Angela's boyfriend called: "It's me. Want to see the new James Bond flick?"

"No. I can't. I promised my dad I'd do the taxes. Call me Sunday."

"OK."

"Bye."

"Bye."

⸺⊸◉⊷⸺

Colors were brilliant. Far more than how they had been reproduced in art books. The sizes of the paintings also came as a surprise. Some were much smaller than Angela expected. Others, larger.

"How do you like this?"

"I love it."

"You know I could never get my boyfriend to come here."

"Your boyfriend?"

"That's just an easy way to refer to him. Say, how about you? I didn't think to ask you if you have a fiancé, girlfriend or if you're married."

"If I was married I wouldn't be getting drafted."

"Is that right?"

"Yes."

"I'd marry you to keep you out of the draft."

"Aren't you sweet."

"I would."

"Sure. A marriage of convenience. What if you met someone or I met someone. How would you explain it."

"Well, I'm sure if they loved us they wouldn't care."

"I suppose not."

"Look at this. It's a Van Gogh."

"I knew that." Robby said.

"You did."

"Sure. If I see a bright painting that looks like a seven year old pressed too hard on his crayons..."

Angela began to laugh.

"And the composition and colors reflect pure genius I would know it is one of his."

"Really, Robby? Whose is this?"

"Toulouse Lautrec."

"How do you know?"

"The poster quality of the work and the subject matter. This is a scene from the Moulin Rouge."

"This?"

"Degas. Ballerinas. Pastels. Bird's eye view looking down."

"Where on earth did you learn this?"

"They made us take art appreciation in high school. My teacher, Mrs. Locke had thousands of pictures from magazines and art books segmented chronologically and by movements. She was great. She had sayings to go along with distinct periods. 'Don't forget Turner,' she would say, 'Turner turned romance into impressionism. But since he was English and early he is not considered part of the movement.'"

"I don't remember you discussing art in San Francisco when we went to the Legion of Honor and Modern Art museums."

"I guess I was a little tongue-tied. I was just a freshman in college, remember. I had all I could do just not to drool in your presence."

<hr>

Robby got lucky and was sent to Frankfurt, Germany his first year of duty. He and Angela stayed in touch. But his re-assignment was Vietnam. He could have avoided the draft, enlisted, and gone in as an officer with his college degree, but he would have had to have served four years. As it was, he was a corporal in the infantry on a two-year hitch.

CHAPTER XVII

1968

PEDRO AND JANINE were in their last semester of college heading toward sheepskins and unofficial degrees in dry-humping. Pants stayed on but Janine's breasts found their way into Pedro's mouth for the grand finale.

Thousands of young Americans, South Vietnamese and Viet Cong had suffered and died while Pedro and Janine were making sparks fly and getting in their last licks before graduating college. The two of them believed less and less in religion, or at least in hell. They rode the wave of the sexual revolution, a little short of completion, losing themselves to the 60s.

Pedro had a night class in Sociology in the springtime. Outside, the fragrance of gardenia hung heavily in the balmy air under a full moon. Leaving class, Pedro bumped into Rick Calderon, a halfMexican-half-black basketball player from East LA who had tears streaming down his face.

"What is it, Rick?"

"Dr. King was shot. He's dead." "Oh Rick. I'm so sorry."

Pedro's generation moved in several directions. There were clean-cut ROTC-types and young Republicans on the one hand and long-haired hippies on the other who smoked pot, dropped acid, and took stands against the war. Some burned their draft cards. They were largely affluent white kids rebelling against the establishment. At odds with their parents. Mainly because their parent's generation had stood up and answered the call to arms. But now, the country was far more divided, to say the least.

War protests became commonplace. Eugene McCarthy, the Democratic Senator from Minnesota announced his candidacy for President on a peace plank vowing to bring home the troops. McCarthy's unexpected success against the sitting president, Lyndon Johnson, in the New Hampshire primary fueled Bobby Kennedy's decision to jump into the race.

Many Democrats, like McCarthy and Kennedy, were increasingly against the war. And not only Democrats, but Americans, in greater numbers, were now against it. Within a few months Johnson held a news conference and shocked the populace by stating that he would neither seek nor accept a nomination from his party for another term as President.

On June 3, 1968, Pedro, at Angela's urging, went to the train station in San Diego to see Bobby Kennedy and listen to his stump speech. Lance Alworth, the San Diego Charger and future football Hall of Famer, was with Kennedy. Both wore dark slacks, Alworth a white shirt, and Kennedy a light blue button down oxford shirt with a striped tie. Kennedy's collar was unbuttoned and his sleeves rolled-up.

"It's time for a change in this country," he said, mopping his auburn, windblown hair from his freckled forehead. He went on — Young people do not need to fight and die, half a world away. Gesturing with his left hand — we need to take care of our own people. By taking care of ourselves we can become a beacon of democracy for others. We cannot export democracy with a gun or a bomb. We have to show the world that our ideas are better, that our people are free, that they are educated, and that they have built a place with their own hands that provides opportunity, not just for some, but for all.

Lance Alworth held onto the shorter, lanky politician, as Kennedy leaned out and shook hands with every last person to approach the platform. Kennedy looked right at Pedro, shook his hand, and smiled, saying in stilted Bostonese, *"Grácias por venir.* Thanks for coming."

Two days later, Pedro saw Kennedy on television, thanking Californians for their votes, after he was declared the winner in the primary, and saying, "It's on to Chicago, let's win there." The Democratic National Convention was set for Chicago in August. Kennedy, with his name and momentum, had picked up enough votes, even with his late entry into the primaries, to be favored for the nomination against McCarthy and the sitting Vice-President, Hubert Humphrey.

Kennedy waved to the crowd, turned and disappeared through a door leading to the hotel kitchen. Television went to commercial. Coming back live, a voice constantly repeated, "Please clear the auditorium." There was alarm and distress in the voice. Pedro turned to his roommate and said, "I bet they shot him." Within moments it was confirmed. Kennedy was shot, in the kitchen of the Ambassador Hotel.

Sirhan Sirhan, a Palestinian immigrant, had fired the shots. Kennedy had a bullet wound to the head. Rafer Johnson, the Olympic Decathlon Gold Medalist, and prominent supporter with the Kennedy party, a live-feed reported, had grabbed Sirhan Sirhan even as he fired shots, and broke Sirhan Sirhan's fingers to pry the gun loose. Other witnesses said Rosy Greer a pro-football player was the one who had taken Sirhan down. Several bystanders were wounded. Authorities were looking for a woman in a polka-dot dress to question.

Assassinations in Dallas, then Memphis, now Los Angeles. A maudlin newscaster stated that the three assassination victims represented the greatest hope for change, equality and democracy in the nation at the time.

Bobbie Kennedy died early the next morning. Pedro had stayed up, glued to the television set, hoping for a miracle.

⸺⸺◉⸺⸺

Pedro and Janine graduated a week later.

⸺⸺◉⸺⸺

Pedro went to work for his father, washing cars and gassing up. He was a lot boy, determined to learn the business from the ground up. That was the only way his father would have let him in.

Pedro spent the summer apart from Janine, who worked in reception, at her parent's small hotel, two blocks from the sands of

Waikiki Beach. Neither Pedro nor Janine had let on anything about their romance to their parents yet the two remained committed to each other. Pedro would come to the islands in the fall for a visit. By that time he expected he would know where he stood with the draft. He no longer had student deferment status and knew it was only a matter of time until he got a draft notice in the mail.

Leo let Angela harangue against the war all she wanted. He agreed with her on certain issues. He did not think that the war served a strategic purpose. Just because it made the military industrial complex whir, and generals happy, it was not enough to convince Leo that kids should risk it all for a far-off country that was basically fighting its own civil war. He had been to war. And he had hoped his son would never have to go. But there would always be proponents of war willing to sacrifice America's sons for a good cause or a bad one.

Getting rid of Hitler was one thing. But Stalin filled the void. The Japanese and the Germans, it seemed to Leo, had learned from the war. They propelled themselves into rebuilding and modernizing their countries. Manufacturing and production were key.

Leo found himself linked to both of these old enemies. He would not have saved the dealerships in 1963 when Studebaker went under if he had not signed franchise contracts with Volkswagen. In 1969 he visited Japan and had his eye on further expansion with Datsun. He liked the Volkswagen and the Datsun because he thought they were better built and more economical than American cars. He really liked Volvos but he did not have the right locations to sell them.

Hovanes' grandson, Aram, was killed in Vietnam. The funeral took place at Fort Rosecrans National Cemetery on Point Loma in San Diego. Hovanes selected the site.

He had seen the cemetery once before, after getting lost on his way to Shelter Island. Driving along Rosecrans Boulevard, he knew he had overshot his turn to Shelter Island, but his natural curiosity led him to follow signs to Cabrillo National Monument. It turned out to be a lighthouse. His wife was still yakking at him for getting lost, while getting out of the car and walking to the hilltop lighthouse with him. There was a stiff breeze on the point where the lighthouse stood.

The view south was spectacular. San Diego Bay, Shelter Island, and the city off to the left. A small mountain cluster beyond. Ahead, Coronado, Silver Strand, the South Bay, and Mexico. A sweeping shoreline divided the land to the left from the vast Pacific Ocean to the right. The El Cortez Hotel, Hotel del Coronado, and Tijuana's Bullring by the Sea could all be seen, along with planes landing and taking off from both the downtown airport, Lindbergh Field, and the North Island Naval Air Station. That day had been crystal clear. The day of the funeral was no different. There was an honor guard, a seven gun salute, a bugler sounded taps, and an American Flag was folded and handed to Aram's mother.

The dead soldier's Great Uncle Ara spoke, breaking into tears along the way, "Aram was a good Armenian-American boy who making his family and his country proud. He serving country well. His Mama and Papa getting a call from his commanding officer who saying he wishing all boys like Aram. Brave and strong. We all sad his life too short. William Saroyan wrote about time of people's life. Let me reading to you: 'In the time of your life live, so that in that wondrous time you shall not add to the misery and sorrow of the world but shall smile to the infinite delight and mystery of it.'

"What can anybody saying about a boy like Aram, you just looking at him, and he making you smile. Full of mischief. Full of promise. Racing round on bicycle, swimming, playing lawn games at barbecues, doing sport in high school, working summers with us. All the good times we having together. God bless our little Aram."

Everyone drove back to Ara's. It had been a long time since Angela and Pedro had been there. They said hello to Antonio, Annee and their children. Then they went to the back wall and looked at the distant city lights, sparkling like the stars in the night they'd replaced.

"Well Pedro, what do think about the war?" asked Angela.

Pedro avoided the question. "Remember coming here when we were kids?"

"Yeah."

"And what about Aram. What an athlete! I always wanted to be on his team for volleyball. We never lost."

"I know. You squirts would take turns spiking the ball a hundred miles an hour at my boobies."

"That was your fault, Angela, you were the only thirteen year old who had 'em."

"I'll probably die of breast cancer, thanks to you and Aram."

"Let's not use the 'd' word if we can avoid it."

"Agreed."

"Speaking of boobies, Aram and I used to watch you and the rest of the girls change into your bathing suits."

"Pedro, that's awful. It's incestuous."

"It wasn't incestuous for Aram... at least where you were concerned."

"Geez, I don't know how to take that revelation."

"It's probably one of Aram's best memories. He always had a crush on you."

"God, I hate seeing all these boys come home in boxes," Angela said.

"Me too."

"So tell me. Didn't you have a little Hawaiian girlfriend?"

"Who said?"

"Joe D'Amico."

"Wait 'til I see him," Pedro's eyes flashed, "tell me about Robby first."

"Robby? Robby got stationed way south in Vietnam. He thinks he won't see much action."

"That's good."

"Are you two an item?"

"What do you mean by that?"

"Are you a couple?"

"Not really."

"If he comes back, what then?"

"I don't know. We'll have to see. Now tell me about Princess Mele Kalikimaka."

"Her name is Janine. She's very sensitive."

"Is she gorgeous?"

"Yes."

"What are you going to do?"

"I don't know. I'm waiting to see if I get drafted."

"You could go in as an officer."

"No. I'd rather do two years than four."

"Why don't you see an orthodontist?"

"What?"

"Get braces on your teeth. It'll keep you out of the Army."

"Are you kidding?"

"No. Craig got braces and they wouldn't take him."

"Did he do it to avoid the draft?"

"No."

"Are you still seeing that guy?"

"On occasion. I told him I met a guy now serving in Vietnam. It really slowed Craig down. Now he feels inadequate with the braces and all. He's a good guy. But I' m trying to let him down easy. Last week I tried to set him up with Elena."

"What's with you and hand-me-downs for your little sister?"

"You're right. I shouldn't."

"Actually, it would be very cruel."

"For whom?"

"Craig, of course."

"Pedro!"

"Well you know Elena. Guys hang around her with their tongues hanging out and she won't give them the time of day."

"I know."

Pedro lifted his glass, "Here's to Aram." Their glasses clinked together, sparkling for an instant, capturing the city lights behind them.

"To Aram, I'm glad he saw my tits."

CHAPTER XVIII

1970

COLONEL DAVID JACKSON worked for the Bureau of Personnel at the Pentagon. He lived in Bethesda, Maryland, and had a driver take him to and from work every day in a grey, late-model Ford, with a government license plate attached to it, and stenciled on the doors of the car in black letters, "USMCBUPERS."

His office was neat. He had a moderately active in-box on his desk and he dealt with special assignments. A memo came across his desk from recruiting.

URGENT: There is a need to step up recruiting in target areas. Decisions regarding a draft lottery and all volunteer army remain on hold. Inner cities and poor rural areas produce many recruits. Need to go into these areas with military veterans who came out of these areas. Seeking recommendations regarding minority veterans' acts of heroism that might have been overlooked. Seeking nominees for medals for bravery. Envision plan of decorating minority veterans and engaging them to speak at high schools, town halls and churches to encourage enlistment.

David Jackson scratched his head. He recalled his war days in the South Pacific, remembering in particular, a Mexican kid from Utah who should have been written up for bravery by Jackson's Commanding Officer (CO) after Jackson's recommendation, but the CO kicked it back.

Jackson began drafting a memo to recruiting, outlining Leo's bravery. That evening Jackson went to the attic of his home and pulled out his old logbook. The next day he transferred the information from his logbook into the memo. He sent it off to recruiting and got an instant response. He was asked to meet with the head of recruiting, General Thompson.

"Thanks for coming in Colonel Jackson."

"Yes, Sir."

"This Leo Figueroa. It's a compelling story."

"Yes, Sir."

"How well is it documented."

"Very well, Sir. I was there. It's in my log."

"You were. Yes, Sir. In fact the plan was mine. Leo was a star athlete, high school graduate from Utah, excellent Marine. It was a remarkable feat."

"But Colonel, what I don't understand, how is it that he never received commendation?"

"I can only give you my opinion, Sir."

"Yes."

"Our CO was a Texan, prejudiced against Mexicans."

"Oh. I see," he said, pausing, then muttering, "Remember the Alamo."

"I guess."

"Well, I don't need to tell you that if everything you say is true that this man should have been recommended for the Navy Cross and Congressional Medal of Honor."

"I agree."

"Colonel, is there some reason why you didn't fight for the commendation."

"I'm sorry to say, Sir, I was primarily concerned with myself. I got a promotion out of the planning of the mission, and other than staying alive, that is all I was looking to do at the time."

"Oh." The explanation was laced with more truth than the General was used to, particularly from a military man hiding in BUPERS during a conflict like Vietnam. "Colonel, do you believe that you sent this boy on a suicide mission?"

"Yes, Sir. I did. I thought he would accomplish some of it, he might make it back. But it was something I personally was not capable of doing and he was the only one I knew who had a chance."

"Colonel, I appreciate your candor."

"Thank you, Sir. It's good to get this out, even now."

"Tell me, did he go back to Utah?"

"I have no idea where he is, or if he is still alive. But I checked his discharge papers. He got out of the service in Los Angeles. He had been married, he had a daughter, and they lived in Hollywood. That was 1945. I remembered him telling me about high school and growing up in Utah."

"Is he Mormon?"

"I doubt it. No. I'm sure he's Catholic."

"More importantly, is he legal?"

"Pardon, Sir."

"A US citizen?"

"Yes. Of course. By birth."

"My goodness. You know Utah has about the smallest percentage of minorities in the country. Can you imagine the impact this man could have on recruiting minorities in Los Angeles. The sheer numbers of Hispanics in that area. He could be a gold mine for us. Let's find him."

"Yes, Sir."

⸻))((((⸻

"Leo, there is a letter here for you from the Marine Corps Bureau of Personnel," Rosa went on, "do you think they put your name on it instead of Pedro's?"

"I don't know. He'd get his Draft Notice from Selective Service, unless maybe the Marines are trying to recruit him as an officer, being a college graduate."

Leo opened the letter.

"Dear Mr. Figueroa: My name is David Jackson. I believe you are the same Leo Figueroa who served as a Marine with me in the campaign for the Marianas in World War II. If I am correct, please contact me at the following telephone number, and feel free to call collect. Please note the three hour time difference. I would like to discuss a commendation that could be bestowed upon you for acts of bravery."

"What does it say?"

"It's some guy I was in the war with. I guess he needs some information."

"About what?"

"I don't know. I'm supposed to call him. What's for dinner?"

"Leftovers."

"Umm, my favorite."

The next day Leo called the Pentagon from work.

"Jackson speaking."

"Colonel, this is Leo Figueroa."

"Leo, great to hear your voice. Thanks for calling."

"Sure."

"I have news for you."

"Yes?"

"Are you sitting down?"

"Yes."

"You are going to be awarded the Congressional Medal of Honor."

"What?"

"It's true. Remember the night you took out the installations with a backpack full of grenades, singlehandedly?"

"Yes."

"Well, that qualifies you for the medal."

"No."

"Yes."

"I don't believe it."

"Believe it. The services have been combing their files for commendations that somehow slipped through the cracks. Like yours did. There will be a ceremony at the White House. You and your family will come to Washington, D.C., all expenses paid. You and I will have some time to catch up. What do you think?"

"I'm shocked."

"What do you do now?"

"I run three auto dealerships. I sell Volkswagens."

"My God you're a success."

"I don't know. I work hard."

"What a great role model."

"I've been lucky."

"Look, Leo, I'll put together a package of information for you and send it to you. Can you come in November?"

"I think so."

"OK. I'll let you know."

"All right."

"Good-bye."

"Good-bye."

Angela, sitting nearby at her desk in the office, had overheard Leo's end of the call. Her father was smiling. Whatever unexpected news he had gotten had to have been a pleasant surprise. His face was beaming.

"What did your Marine buddy have to say, Papa?"

"He said I'm getting the Congressional Medal of Honor."

Angela's head leaned involuntarily toward her father, her jaw dropped, and her eyes went wide.

———— ◈ ————

At dinner, Leo told the story of the night he took out the installations. He omitted the hand-to-hand killings and running naked.

"That was a brave mission, Pop," Pedro said, "I'm surprised Elena and I are here to hear about it. You deserve a medal. We're proud of you, Pop."

"Who have you told?" Rosa asked.

"Just you."

"Wait 'til the Avakians hear. Expect a major publicity campaign. Ford and Chevy will be calling to give you dealerships. There will be a big article in the 'LA Times' and in 'La Opinion,' 'Time Magazine,' 'Newsweek,' there will be something on the local and national TV news, I bet. You'll be famous. You'll finally get to throw a pitch at Dodger Stadium."

"Look. I'm honored. More than honored. But I don't want to parlay this into anything. The way I remember it, brave people died."

"It's inevitable, Leo," said Rosa. "They'll want you to join the VFW. Everyone will want to shake your hand, buy you a drink. Remember that Cherokee Indian who raised the flag at Iwo Jima, drank himself to death and drowned in a puddle of rainwater on a reservation somewhere in Oklahoma, I think?"

"Yeah. That's why I don't want this to change my life." "We're so proud of you, Daddy," Elena said.

All the hubbub and commotion started once Ara found out, and it did not let up heading into November.

"What's wrong, Papa? I've never seen you so glum?" Angela asked one morning at work.

"Angela, I have listened to you voice your negative opinion about the war since it started. You don't believe Lee Harvey Oswald acted alone and you want the troops out now. You campaigned for John Kennedy and Robert Kennedy and stood on Pennsylvania Avenue to see the coffin when the first one was shot, and stood in the ballroom of the Ambassador Hotel the night the second one was shot. You don't trust the government and you hate Richard Nixon and despise Henry Kissinger even more.

"Your Papa, some brown guy from LA, is going to shake their hands, pose with them for the cameras, and make them look like they care about us Mexicans as human beings rather than fodder for their wars. How do you think I feel? I feel like I'm letting my kids down. Do you think I want to see Pedro drafted? Or Robby come home in a box?"

Angela broke in, "I'm surprised you remember his name."

"I'm your Papa. Of course I do. And he's a damn good kid."

"So, Papa. What is it?"

"I have to go get this thing, take it into my hands, for every last Mexican-American in this country. But I don't want any of them going off to Vietnam because of me."

The next week the Figueroas went to DC.

Colonel Jackson spoke to Leo: "I've taken some time out of your schedule so you and I can go to the Officer's Club and have a little chat about something that should interest you."

"Sure."

They sat in a red leather booth at the Officers Club facing the bar, across the way, painted in black enamel and outfitted with brass. A Filipino in a white starched jacket with gold buttons and black pants atop shiny black shoes stood at attention next to their table and very politely asked what he could get for them.

"Martini, extra dry for me. Leo?"

"I'll have a Coke."

"That's the difference, I guess, between Medal of Honor recipients and the rest of us military."

"I'll have a beer from time to time, but with everything going on I want to keep a clear head."

"Good call, Leo. You know, we would like you to make some appearances for the Marines. How would you like a stipend of say $50,000 to make appearances in California, Arizona and Texas to about 50 high schools and churches. We'll pick up all your travel costs, too. It will give you an opportunity to connect with your people and encourage the young men to consider the military. It's a hell of a good thing for them. Get them out of poverty, away from gangs, and into the mainstream. You know."

"Generous offer, Colonel. But level with me. What do you think of this war?"

"Truth?"

"Yes."

"It's not winnable unless we bomb the hell out of Hanoi, Haiphong and the rest of the North."

"Did you read that article, it was in the LA Times, from the guy at the Rand Corporation who believes bombing only emboldens the enemy?"

"No. I didn't see that one."

"These people have nothing except the notion that their own little plot of ground is worth fighting and dying for. It's kill or be killed for them. If we stay and keep pouring money and lives into a lost cause we're foolish. I thought Korea would be the end of fighting for the US in Asia."

"Well Leo, I'm sure it's all more complicated than you or I can imagine."

"You work at the Pentagon, Colonel. How complicated can it be for you?"

"So what are you telling me, Leo, you are a Medal of Honor recipient and a conscientious objector rolled into one?"

The drinks arrived.

"No. I'm saying there is a vast difference between a global and regional conflict. In a global conflict the participants have no choice but to fight, unless of course they're French. The Colonel, who had just taken the first sip of his martini, interrupted Leo with a hearty laugh, uncontrollably baptizing Leo in martini spray. Leo laughed too, daubing his face with a napkin, then continued, serious again, "But in my book the French got it right — they lost an entire generation in their home fields during World War I, at the Somme and along the Maginot Line — I don't blame them a bit for World War II — they were the only enlightened nation in the group — anyway, in a regional conflict, it is up to the rest of the world not to participate, to make sure that the conflict does not expand beyond the region."

"Not that simple, Leo. What if our national security depends on the stability of a region?"

"Our national security should depend on our ability to defend ourselves not to wage campaigns thousands of miles from our own soil."

"What if we need the natural resources of a country to compete economically or militarily?"

"Like oil, say, like what prompted Japan to attack us, once we cut off its oil?"

"Exactly."

"Then with all of the intelligence and strength, both economic and military, we are better off developing alternate energy sources, or taking a small portion of the millions of dollars going into the military to be used to modify the internal combustion engine to the extent gas mileage is increased five, ten or fifty-fold. It can be done. Electric cars are just around the corner."

"But to keep from waging war on our own soil don't we have to wage it elsewhere?" the Colonel continued.

"I don't think so. I don't think the winner of North Vietnam versus South Vietnam is going to get on boats to attack the West Coast or launch a single missile. Colonel, don't ask me to recruit minority kids to fight a war that makes multi-national corporations richer, and feeds the military-industrial complex that Ike, whom I liked, warned us against. These kids, the military wants to exploit, don't have the vote and can't even buy beer."

"We all liked Ike."

"And you know why?" Leo did not wait for an answer, "because he was a soldier and he knew war. I was a Marine and I knew it too. Vietnam is not a war that the US should be fighting. It has regional implications. When the Chinese start shooting at us then we should shoot back."

"It may be too late."

"If we ever engage them it will already be too late. We need leaders with vision. It's time to stop destroying ourselves and build peaceful coalitions."

"That's contrary to human nature, isn't it Leo?"

"We need to change our nature then. Or we won't survive."

"Leo, are you going to engage the President and Secretary of State with your theories on global peace when you meet with them?"

"If they ask. I certainly haven't put any of this into an acceptance speech for the medal ceremony tomorrow, if that's what worries you."

The Colonel eyed a man coming into the club. "Leo, I've enjoyed our conversation."

The man had silver hair. He wore a navy blue suit, white shirt, and champagne colored tie. He had a military bearing. There was something about him that reminded Leo of someone.

"Right on time," Colonel Jackson said.

"Because of the snow storm, I had to take the train from New York, but I still made it," the man said to the Colonel. Turning to Leo, he said, "Remember me, Leo?"

"Mickey?"

Colonel Jackson had arranged for Mickey McGonigle to tag along. Mickey had read of the medal recipients in the New York Times and wanted the chance to see Leo again. They never stayed in touch like they told each other they would. After a few phone calls Mickey had gotten through to the Colonel and asked if he could come to DC to meet Leo.

At the White House dinner, there were two other medal recipients and their families in attendance, along with the Congressmen and Senators from the recipients' home states, and members of the armed forces committees.

After dinner, Rosa sent Leo and Mickey off alone in a cab to Georgetown where the cabby took them to a piano bar where they could have a drink and catch up.

Leo went straight to the men's room. Meanwhile Mickey found a table and took out a gold Cross ball-point pen, he had previously given to one of his sons when he graduated high school, and wrote on a napkin, "Please play 'Marine Hymn' for Leo Figueroa. He's here. Tomorrow he gets the Congressional Medal of Honor at the White House."

Mickey carefully turned the pen top to retract the point and put the pen in his shirt pocket before giving the waitress the napkin and a twenty dollar bill. The piano player was finishing "Misty" and moving onto "More" by the time Leo found the booth with Mickey in it.

"What did you think of the President?" Mickey asked when Leo sat down.

Leo responded, "His wife is extremely nice, the girls and their husbands seemed very nice, too. Him, I don't trust."

"He couldn't've carried water for our baseball team in WESPAC. He looks like he should be handing out towels in a whorehouse. The son of a bitch is ruining this country."

"Geez, Mick. I didn't think I'd hear something like that from a distinguished veteran like yourself."

"Damnit, Leo. I didn't want to tell you, but I lost both my sons in this goddamned war."

"Mickey."

"I got a divorce after that. Everything we worked for, our whole lives, down the tubes."

"I'm sorry, Mickey."

"Look, Leo, I don't want to rain on your parade. I'm so proud of you. No one deserves the medal more than you do. Why the jarheads waited so long to give it to you is a mystery to me."

"It's a publicity stunt. They want me to recruit minority kids to fight this war."

"Jesus Christ. Are you going along with it?"

"I'm not going to do it. I told them today I wouldn't."

"You still get the medal, don't you?"

"Sure."

"And, I mean it. You deserve it."

"Thanks."

"What a great looking family you have."

"Thanks."

Mickey went on, "I thought Angela was going to throw up with Nixon hovering over her, arms folded, rocking on his heels, like that. Fumbling with small talk."

"She hates him."

"What about your boy, Pedro? What's his draft status?"

"Just graduated college, lost his '2 S' deferment, he'll be classified '1 A' any minute."

"Anything physical that would keep him out?"

"No."

"Does he want to go?"

"No."

"Can you pull any strings?"

"I think Colonel Jackson would help me if I asked. But I can't bring myself to ask. Anyway, I think Jackson would trade Pedro for me going out to high schools and churches and telling them what a great opportunity joining up would hold."

"He's your only boy, Leo. I encouraged my boys to go in. It was the biggest mistake of my life."

Leo put his head down for a moment. Looking up he said, "Your best days Mickey?" "When they were little."

"Me too."

The waitress returned with the twenty, slipped it into Mickey's hand and whispered in his ear, "It's on the house." Mickey pushed it back into her hand and told her to keep it.

The piano player played a soft piece. It was a delightful introduction to a familiar, yet unrecognizable tune to most in the crowd, that only hinted, after a few more bars, at something familiar. By the time he went full volume with it, it was unmistakably "The Marine Hymn." Several people in the crowd hit their feet and sang along.

"Always liked the leathernecks," Mickey confided in Leo, who had remained seated.

The piano player leaned close to the microphone and said, "That was for Leo Figueroa who's getting the Congressional Medal of Honor tomorrow."

Leo leaned toward Mickey, raising his voice above the applause, "Mickey, how could you?"

"Take a bow, Leo."

Leo stood and waved. Soon Mickey's and Leo's table was filled with complimentary drinks from around the room and several people came over, congratulated Leo and shook his hand. Then a man with a scowl came over and said, "You can shove that medal up your ass. We're killing babies in Vietnam."

"I'm sorry, son."

"Really? You shoulda served in my unit." There was a look of horror in the young man's eyes.

"It's war, son," Mickey said in a fatherly tone.

"Fuck off, old man," the intruder said, dispensing with both of them.

"He's right," Mickey said. "Let's go."

They stood up. "It's so good to see you Mickey."

⸺◈⸺

Word trickled up from USMCBUPERS that Leo would not play ball with the Pentagon on recruitment. The White House was informed.

⸺◈⸺

It was not long before Pedro received his draft notice, and papers to report for physical, both in the same envelope from the Selective Service Commission. He called Janine. "Pedro, what are you going to do?"

"I don't know. My dad said I should apply for pilot training in the Navy. I met a World War II pilot, Commander McGonigle, a friend of my dad's, when we went for my dad's medal ceremony at the White House. He told me that Navy flight training at Pensacola, Florida was taking thirteen months. But even before that the application process for an officer candidate would take at least four months. Once I apply, the Selective Service process halts, and takes a back seat to the Navy application. Assuming they take me, worst case, my first assignment, after training, comes sometime in late 1971. Commander McGonigle told me, 'With all the campaign promises to get us out of Vietnam, and the Vietnamization plan, I should never see combat because the war should be over before I finish training.' I would still have to serve for four years, but flying, he says, and I believe him, is an excellent career. Then I could get a job with an airlines, fly cargo, fly fixed wing tours over the Grand Canyon, teach flying, or maybe get a job doing helicopter tours in Hawaii."

"I'm all for that. Still coming to Hawaii?"

"Yes."

"I can't wait."

"Me, neither. I love you Janine."

"Te quiero, Pedro."

⸻ ◆ ⸻

Leo went to Utah by himself. "Hi, Papa."

"Leo! What a surprise. Congratulations!"

"I had to see you. I wish you would have come with us to Washington. You could have met the President."

"I hope you gave him a swift boot in the ass for me," after a slight comedic pause, Pedro continued,"you know we aren't much for traveling. I hope you don't feel like we let you down."

"Oh, no, Papa."

"Well, we are very proud of you. Always been proud of you. You're a good boy, Leo. Good husband. Good provider. Hard worker."

"OK, Papa. Thanks."

"I mean it, Leo."

"Well, Papa. I get it all from you and Mama."

"Yeah, and you give it to your kids. Your Mama be home soon."

"Where is she?"

"Doctor's."

"Anything wrong?"

"She's real tired all the time."

"That doesn't sound good."

"We'll see... what are you doing here?"

"I told myself, first chance I get, I'm going home and give this medal to my parents."

"Leo, come on, it's yours. Put it in your house where everyone can see it."

"Is Eddy around?"

"Sure. I think he's in the barn."

<hr />

Leo and Eddy shook hands and gave each other bear hugs. "So let's see it, Leo."

Leo pulled the box from his pocket and handed it to Eddy. Eddy opened it. "Wow, Leo, that's great. How come you never told us about this?"

"How come you never told me about carrying the bomb?"

"You mean critical components for the first one?"

"Yeah."

"I never knew it for a long time afterward. Anyway, even if I had known, I didn't need any more reminders of that ship or its crew. I was fine with holding onto my own memories. I found them a burden. I wasn't going to unload them on anybody else."

"I guess I wasn't either."

"Anyway, congratulations. I guess we can both say we saved lives by killing people."

"Yep."

They pondered Eddy's wisdom for a moment.

"Eddy, how's my mom?"

"I don't know, Leo. She's slowing down a little."

<hr />

"Hi, Mama!"

"Leo! What are you doing here?" He hugged and kissed her.

"I came to surprise you and show you the medal. I wanted to leave it with you and Papa but he said I should keep it."

"You should."

"So how are you feeling?"

"Oh. Just a little tired. They took my blood and will have the results in a few days."

"You'll be fine, Mama."

———=⟨◉⟩=———

Leo returned to LA. He got a call that his mother's white blood cell count was not good. She had cancer. It was spreading. She had a matter of months. During that time, Leo made as many trips to Utah as he could. Toward the end, he took a vacation and spent the last ten days with his dying mother and the rest of the family.

On her last day she was unconscious and medicated for pain. She had an I-V. The arm receiving the I-V drip was cold to the touch. Leo stroked her forehead, then moved away from the bedside for others to come up and pay their respects. When she took her last breath everyone around her broke down.

After she was buried Leo asked his father if he wanted to come to LA for a visit. He declined.

That spring Pedro spent a lot of time in Teresa's gardens, growing vegetables, tending to Teresa's roses, and producing a little crop of strawberries, about half the output Teresa would get.

———=⟨◉⟩=———

Janine stood outside Gate 2 at Honolulu Airport wearing salmon-colored, floral patterned shorts, a white brocade tube top and tan leather sandals. It was windy, and strands of her hair fluttered beneath a white visor. United Flight 50 from Los Angeles had touched down and was taxiing toward her. When the plane stopped a staircase on wheels was rolled up to it and secured near the door, which opened.

Passengers disembarked. Janine glanced at each one momentarily, then the next. When she saw Pedro she clasped her hands and jumped up. She waved, and he waved back.

"Before we go home," she said, "I can show you a few sights. Or, we can go straight home. Or if you are hungry, I can take you for some food."

"Or," he said, "we should get this over with first."

"What?"

"Meeting your parents."

"OK. You're right."

<hr>

Janine's mother and father cornered her early the next morning. "Janine," her father said, "he seems like a nice boy but this whole thing about timing his entry into the Navy to avoid Vietnam. I don't like that, Janine."

"Dad, why should he go over there and die for nothing?"

"Let's not get so dramatic. I'm just saying that he does not seem to have convictions. It shows me he's weak."

"Are we really having this conversation?"

"What?"

"You don't even know him and already you don't like him."

"I didn't say that. Look, it's OK to have a boyfriend but before you get serious with him or anyone else you need to know what kind of a person he is. You're brother wouldn't have looked for loopholes to avoid serving if he were alive."

"Dad. How can you even talk about Denny?"

"Because no son of mine would look for loopholes. He would do his duty, just like I did."

"Pedro's father won a Congressional Medal of Honor for God's sake."

"You don't win them, you get them for extraordinary valor."

"Well, he got it."

"That doesn't make him anything like his father."

"This war is not World War II. My generation would have done just what yours did if we were alive during World War II, and yours would be doing the same thing mine is now."

"It's no different, Janine. Duty is duty. And cowards are cowards." The dialogue had lit fuses on both sides.

"All right, dad. You want him out of here fine. He and I are off to do some sightseeing. Now I think, we'll sail to Maui for a couple days."

"I'm warning you, Janine. If you go to Maui with that boy, don't come back."

Janine walked out and her father turned to her mother, saying, "A fortune for her college education and she brings home a Mexican."

The mother responded in a tone of disgust, "I don't know why you marry me. You got what you deserve. You want her stateside to stay away from Hawaiian surfer crowd. You always looking for a howlie for her."

<hr>

"Pedro, I don't know how to say this but I got in a fight with my father."

"Over me?"

"Yeah."

"So?"

"He told me he didn't think you had convictions and you shouldn't be looking for ways to avoid fighting in the war."

"Christ, Janine, I'm joining the goddamned Navy, I'm putting in four years, I'll be taking off with bombs in tow and landing on aircraft carriers in the middle of the ocean. Doesn't that count for anything with him?"

"That's not it. He's still fighting World War II. For him, it's America, love it or leave it."

"Well, what do you want me to do?"

"I don't know. You can get to know him better. Talk to him."

"Don't you think he took one look at me and made up his mind?" She nodded.

"So?"

"So, I got mad at him and told him that you and I were going off alone for a couple days to Maui..."

"That sounds great."

"But. He told me if I did, don't come back."

"Geez, Janine. You know, we planned this visit all wrong. It would have been better if I stayed somewhere else and you told him you were off with your girlfriend somewhere."

"I couldn't do that to them."

"You never kept anything from them?"

His question brought up the unspeakable between them.

"Look, Pedro. This is nonsense. You came here to have a good time. We've been planning this for a long time. I won't see you again for who knows how long. I can't believe we are having this discussion."

"I can't either. But your dad, apparently, has it in for me."

"I think, down deep, he likes you, but he's afraid you might take me away from him."

"He *don't* like me. Period. For whatever reason."

"So what should we do?"

"Get on with our vacation. Stay on Oahu and avoid your father at all costs."

"Then let's get a room today." Janine was serious. "It'll have to be some place where they don't know me."

"How many places know you?"

"I don't mean that. Look almost everyone in the hotel business knows everyone else. My family's been in the business all my life. We'll get a place in Haleiwa."

———— ◦◉◦ ————

Pedro made no headway with Mr. Dugan during his stay. But Pedro left Hawaii feeling he had gotten the upper hand. He and Janine had finally gone all the way and then some, on an unforgettable afternoon in a light tropical rain on a cool tile balcony overlooking Sunset Beach.

———— ◦◉◦ ————

Pedro had taken the written examination to become a Navy pilot.

He passed. Then he took a stringent flight physical, and passed it. He awaited notification, and papers he would need to sign, to report to Pensacola and flight school.

Meanwhile, a Draft Lottery was announced. Three hundred sixty-six dates, one for each day of the year, would get written on ping pong balls and go into an air hopper, including February 29, the leap year date. As each date was pulled from the hopper, it would get a number from 1, for the first date pulled, to 366, the last date pulled. Based on the number of eligible draftees, the government had already concluded that it would need draftees from the first 125 numbers pulled, to meet the draft quota that year.

The same process would be repeated each year thereafter. So if a draft eligible male's birthday was among the first 125 he would likely get drafted. Anyone higher would likely avoid being drafted, and no one would be submitted to any more than one lottery. If a person was not drafted in the year he participated in the lottery, he could not be drafted after that.

So the higher the number the less the likelihood of getting drafted. That first year the military ended up drafting males whose birthdays corresponded to the first 115 dates pulled from the hopper.

Pedro's birth date was chosen number 361 out of 366. There was no way he would get drafted. He immediately contacted the Navy and withdrew his name from consideration for flight training.

He also called Janine but got her father on the phone. Mr. Dugan was surprised to hear from him. Pedro had no inkling of the activities surrounding the Dugan household.

"Janine is not here. Who is this?"

"Pedro Figueroa."

"Oh."

"When will she be in?"

"I guess she didn't tell you," he paused, "of course why would she?"

"Tell me what?"

"She eloped a week ago. She married an Italian from Switzerland." The news was shocking. For some reason Mr. Dugan kept talking, "After the honeymoon, they'll be living in Europe."

Pedro had nothing to say but managed a "Thanks, Mr. Dugan."

"Sure."

Pedro wrestled with images of Janine, both plain and provocative. She had broken his heart.

Again.

◦◦◦

Pedro did not want to sell cars. He wanted to get away. He thought it was time to go to graduate school. He had majored in business and minored in Spanish. He applied for the Masters Program at the University of New Mexico in Spanish and got accepted.

But before that, he and Joe D'Amico, who had stayed out of the Army with bad knees, left for Alaska. Joe had an old Dodge station wagon whose power brakes went out on a curvy mountain road fifty miles out of Eugene, Oregon. Fortunately, the boys soon found out, the brakes worked if you pressed down as hard as you could with two feet, even without the power assist. The boys had the car fixed in Eugene and drove on to Seattle. Unemployment there was at 22%. Boeing had laid off countless workers. And heading into spring, even jobs in Alaska were looking scarce.

Pedro and Joe took the ferry to Ketchikan along the inland waterway. Joe got seasick. Pedro didn't. They drank beer in the bar. Rainier Beer. And talked to others headed north for work. There was Jake Law, father of two, laid off from Boeing. He had logged after high school, some fifteen years before.

"Logging is the hardest thing I ever did. Make you strong as an ox. It'll put muscles in your shit."

He wasn't kidding. Thanks to Jake's tales, Pedro and Joe had learned enough logging lingo to carry on a conversation with the owner of a logging camp, looking for men, after coming up two short on Easter Sunday. He had two empty seats on an old Army Mule aircraft, affixed with pontoons, fueled and ready to take off for Williams Logging Camp in Whale Pass.

"Where you boys from?"

"California."

"What have you done?"

"Worked for Weyerhaueser in Northern California, two and half years." A big fat lie.

"High lead? Cat?"

"Cat, but we're ready for high lead."

"You're not fairies, are you? Coming from California?"

"Hell no!"

"OK, you're on. Get your gear and meet me at that plane over there in a half hour."

"Thanks."

The boys were living the dream. They took off from the water, climbed over mountains and looked down on dense forest in the Alaskan panhandle. After an hour they set down amid a couple of splashes on a high mountain lake in Whale Pass, taxied to the dock, stepped out, and pulled their gear from the plane. When the engine sputtered to a stop the whole place went quiet and serene. The boys' hearts were in their throats.

It was nearly dark. The boys were shown their bunks, across from each other in a long narrow bunkhouse, twenty-four bunks in all, then taken to the General Store where cash was no good. They were charged for several items, including caulks, black rugged work boots with spikes in the soles. Old hands told them to soak the caulks overnight in transmission fluid to help wear them in. The boys opted to take their chances on blisters.

The evening meal was in the mess hall. Several kinds of salad, steak, potatoes, carrots, milk, coffee, tea, and pie and ice cream for dessert.

"Go get seconds," one of the old timers said. "They charge you by the meal, might as well make it worth your while."

Food became sacred to the boys. After a week they were going back for three and four helpings. The mountains, air, and hard work gave them enormous appetites. Breakfast, a half-dozen pancakes, four eggs, six slices of bacon, several sausage links, orange juice and milk; lunch; six sandwiches with cold cuts, chips and fruit, and more milk; dinner, four steaks, a couple chickens, or a dozen slices of ham, seven or eight glasses of milk, pounds of potatoes, vegetables, three servings of dessert and all the fruit, for later, that they could stuff into their pockets.

In two weeks Pedro went from 147 lbs. to 172 lbs., all muscle. Despite the weight gain, his waist went from 29" to 26 1/2." For Joe it was the same.

The work took all the boys' strength and each ounce of energy. They walked up and down fallen logs, constantly suffered the pain of having their shins smashed against all sorts of underbrush. They lost their footing on occasion and fell ten to fifteen feet into melting snow or scratchy ground cover. They dragged hundreds of pounds of cable up and down mountainsides. Joe's knees held up but hurt every day.

The snow had been up to their hips when they started the day after Easter. When it warmed up a little, and the snow melted, *noseeums* came out at dusk — black, swarming, barely-visible flies that bite.

The boys wore aluminum helmets, shaped like the ones from World War I, woolen Long-Johns, tin (logging) pants, suspenders, black and white striped shirts, like Casey Jones, and cotton gloves. Always a neckerchief.

When the green painted police plane flew over, several of their co-workers ducked for cover. It was anyone's guess what they had done, where they had done it, or who was after them.

The boys were choker-setters. It was their job to wrap steel cables around one, two or three logs at a time, depending on the diameters of the downed trees and if they were laying close enough together to wrap in the same choker. The chokers were in pairs, each with a steel knob, on the end of the cable, that fit into a loose steel collar that slid up and down the cable. Tension on the cable, once wrapped around a log, with the sliding collar coupled to the steel knob, secured the massive load.

The job did not hold the risk of combat but of the 234 loggers who logged that year 13 died in logging accidents. Joe nearly got decapitated when a cable caught on the top of a pecker pole (small tree) then whipsawed within inches of his head. Pedro had to jump out of the way of a huge hemlock that fell unexpectedly toward him in a thunderous crash that shook the ground around him.

⟞⟨◉⟩⟝

The money Pedro earned logging allowed him to spend the summer after his first year in graduate school in Salamanca, Spain, studying Spanish at the University. It was a golden city from the color of the stone used to build it centuries before. There was a two-thousand year old Puente Romano (Roman Bridge) over the River Tormes where Lazarillo de Tormes of Picaresque novel fame, learned the hard way, never to trust anyone. And a huge Cathedral, under repair.

When classes ended, Pedro bought a EU-RAIL pass and went to Lisbon then Paris with a girl he had met in summer school. She was from the University of Missouri. Really nice with a good head on her shoulders. But Pedro never saw her again once he got back to the States.

⟞⟨◉⟩⟝

When Robby came home from Vietnam he and Angela got a place in Silver Lake. A small rental on Lucille. They announced to their parents that they were *not* getting married but were going to live together.

"You're both adults. You should get married. But we can't make you," came the parental reply. Still both sets of parents got together and took their shameless kids to the Captain's Table on La Cienega for dinner to celebrate their non-marriage. The *maître d'*, in a rich baritone voice, honed from years in Hollywood, crooned a beautiful "Welcome to the Captain's Table" to them as they entered the restaurant.

Robby got a job teaching history at Wilson High School. He wanted to return to the Bay Area but Angela convinced him to stay in LA. As far as finances, Angela was the Assistant Manager of the dealerships under her father and made more money than Robby. She encouraged Robby to go back to school. He toyed with the idea of a doctorate in history. Angela told him to get a law degree.

Robby enrolled at a night school in West Los Angeles called Los Angeles Western School of Law. The school was housed in a converted warehouse section of a Ralph's Supermarket on Wilshire where a half dozen class rooms had been partitioned. The owners of the school were both lawyers, a man and his son. Tuition was the lowest in the State. There were a majority of minority students in attendance. Robby was able to get through without having to take out a loan.

In California a person could get a license to practice law by passing the bar. It did not matter if the person graduated from an accredited law school, an unaccredited law school, like Robby's, or if he was mentored in a law firm. Those, not from accredited law schools, however, had to take and pass a "baby bar" exam before they could sit for the real bar exam.

CHAPTER XIX

1972

ONE MORNING WHEN Angela was at local campaign headquarters for George McGovern, in the days in early June leading up to the California primary, she got nauseous and went into the bathroom to splash some cold water on her face. Scrawled next to the mirror in pencil on a wall wearing a greying shade of yellow paint was: "Don't switch Dicks in the middle of a screw, vote for Nixon in '72."

It looked like Robby's handwriting. She could not wait to call him on it. For a moment there, she was laughing aloud from the graffiti; the next, she was throwing up in the sink.

Angela was pregnant.

But she lost the baby in the fourth month. Doctors suggested a number of tests that she ended up taking. There was nothing to show why she had lost the baby or if she would be at risk in a future pregnancy. All they could say was that it was one of those things.

<hr>

News outlets on June 17, 1972 reported a break-in at the offices of the Democratic National Committee in Washington, DC in the early morning hours.

It turned out the Republicans were spying on the Democrats. But that was not enough to get the peace candidate, George McGovern, elected. Nixon was still at war and the American electorate held on to him in a landslide.

By the following summer the so-called Watergate Hearings began. White House counsel, John Dean, testified before a Congressional committee that he'd told President Nixon that there was a cancer growing on the presidency. Dean was referring to the cover-up of the break-in of Watergate that the White House was actively engaged in. A criminal conspiracy right in the White House. Sordid characters emerged. When the pieces began falling into place it appeared that Nixon had known about the planning of the Watergate break-in, and he and his closest advisors, J.R. Haldeman, John Erlichman, and the Attorney General of the United States, John Mitchell, had tried to keep a lid on Watergate. By the next year Nixon faced impeachment, but, before the final vote was taken, he opted for resignation. It was a mercenary decision. Had he been impeached he would have lost his pension.

⚯

It had taken Robby four years at night to get his law degree. During the last year of law school he answered a messenger ad for a law firm in Beverly Hills, and stopped teaching. The firm, Shapiro, Mason & Hughes specialized in banking and real estate law. Robby got hired as a messenger to file documents, serve subpoenas and deliver correspondence throughout Southern California. After six months, the managing partner, Henry Hughes, offered Robby a job as a paralegal. Robby began to draft legal documents, summarize depositions and research motions.

The firm was expanding and it looked like there would be a job for him once he passed the bar. But Robby went to a not-for-profit legal aid organization, run on donations, called Justice Now. It opened its doors to clients of every racial and religious background. Its goal was to make a difference in the lives of the most vulnerable members of the community.

Robby and Angela struggled along, mostly on her salary since much of Robby's initial time at Justice Now was chalked up as volunteer. They put off having children. By year's end Robby started making a decent living. No sooner did that happen than Angela quit the dealerships and went to work at Justice Now where her Spanish allowed her to interview clients and keep them informed while their cases made their way slowly through the legal system.

"Papa," she had said, "I'm sorry but I want to work with Robby at Justice Now. I'll stay as long as you need me but I've made up my mind."

"You know, Angela, I had always hoped that you would take my job once I retire."

"I know, Papa."

"I want you to know, *m'ija* (my daughter) I not only respect your decision, I admire it."

She hugged him tightly.

———◦((◦))◦———

Pedro taught ESL (English as a Second Language) in LA at the English Language Institute on Commonwealth, after he got his Masters. The majority of students were Iranian, studying in the US on oil money from their families back home. Pedro had his eye on several of the girls but knew they could get planted waist-deep in dirt and pummeled to death with rocks and he could end up in a bad way if he flirted with them.

The job hardly paid and Pedro was thinking of going back for a doctorate. He rented a place with Joe D'Amico in the old neighborhood. Joe worked for an insurance company on the Miracle Mile and was taking computer classes at night.

The phone rang and Pedro answered.

"Pedro?"

"Yes."

"It's Janine. Please don't hang up."

"Where are you?"

"I'm in Santa Barbara."

"What's going on, Janine?"

"I want to see you?"

"Aren't you married?"

"We're getting a divorce."

"Where is he?"

"Geneva."

"Sorry, Janine. Not this time." He hung up.

The phone rang. "Hello."

"Please Pedro." The sobbing sounded real. He could envision the tears, the runny nose, the whole thing. "I think I'm going to kill myself."

"Not if you find someone else, Janine. You know you are quite resilient."

"I mean it, Pedro."

"I don't believe you."

"I'm at the Goleta Resort and Spa on Coast Highway, number 11." She hung up.

It was nine-thirty, Friday night. She was two hours away. He told himself he was only going there for closure.

He got there at quarter to twelve. It was an easy drive. Not much traffic. Cool evening. A nice trip, with the car window rolled down and the smell of the ocean for the last half-hour.

He found the spa and knocked on number 11. No answer. He waited and knocked again. He thought about breaking the door down to rescue her when the door cracked open. Light fell across a portion of her face. Strands of loose hair glistened."I fell asleep. Give me a minute."

She finally opened the door, hair in place, wearing only a nightgown. Tangerine. Sheer. See-through. "Oh Pedro." She put her arms around him and set her face in that old familiar position against his neck. She smelled the same. Looked the same.

"Pedro. Make me pregnant," she said. "I want your baby. I never should have left you."

"What are you saying?"

"Pedro, I got pregnant when you came to Hawaii. I had an abortion. I couldn't tell you." Pedro was too stunned to reply. "I knew you would want to get married. I wasn't ready for it. When I met Claudio I didn't want to marry him but I had to get away from my father. So I did. I thought Claudio could make me happy. But he couldn't. Only you can."

Pedro had braced himself for anything, but not quite this."I don't know what's wrong with you, Janine. I used to love you from the top of your head to the bottom of your toes and everything in between. But that head of yours. And I guess that heart of yours is so fickle... you know, I, I'm just better off without you. I can't believe you'd do that to a baby, either."

"I was crazy, Pedro. I know. But now, I know it can work. I went away because I don't deserve you. You're good. I'm not. But I think I understand some things now that I didn't before."

"I'm not so good."

"Pedro, I love you. I want to have a baby with you. I want to raise a family."

"Janine, we're both messed up. I don't know what I'll end up doing. You're bouncing between continents and men and what you think you want. Your track record stinks. I'm sorry, Janine. I got off the roller coaster with you and I just don't want to get back on. Flattering as it may be that you always come back to me, that still makes me the guy you always leave."

Pedro had been fortifying himself for the big turn down all the way from LA to Santa Barbara and nothing was going to change his mind.

She refused to believe him on nearly every level. But he would not budge.

"OK. Go then." She rearranged her nightgown as she spoke and straightened her spine. He kept eye contact with her, refusing to be blinded by the curves, the rosy orbs, or the mink-to-the-touch curls below the navel. All there for the taking. He turned to the door and opened it.

"Pedro?"

He went through the door before turning round, "Get your life straightened out," he said, taking all of her in, "then call me. We'll see." He closed the door behind him.

He drove back to LA wondering what he had done and if he had really let go. Mainly he felt sad for both Janine and the baby.

CHAPTER XX

1977

GUILLERMO AUGUSTIN FIRST shook hands with Angela at a Chicano Awards Banquet sponsored by the Los Angeles Chamber of Commerce. The banquet was held at the new Bonaventure Hotel. Augustin had a room there and no one to share it with. He did not realize that Angela had come with Robby who was yakking it up with other lawyers in attendance.

Guillermo was from San Francisco and worked on a committee to identify and support Hispanic political candidates throughout California. He had graduated from Harvard and understood demographics. He had a master plan and a map to go with it. He was handsome as hell.

He stood before Angela and several other Latin women, drinking and chatting. One ran an ESL program for CETA. Another was a local news personality. And the other, was the ignored wife of a wealthy building contractor. Everyone was formally attired. Guillermo knew his best chance for a partner that evening was the contractor's wife. Every word out of her mouth had sexual overtones and her husband was out of town on business. But Guillermo wanted Angela.

Over time Guillermo's audience dwindled down to just her. It was obvious to the other women which one of them he was trying to impress. Guillermo kept returning the topic to Angela's father, after the newswoman had offered up that Angela's father had received the Congressional Medal of Honor.

"Is he here tonight?"

"No."

"Does he ever come to functions like this?"

"No."

"Is he introverted?"

"No. I wouldn't say so."

"How's his English?"

"Flawless, really. Not even an accent. If that's what you are getting at."

"Is he political?"

"No. But he knows politics. He has read the LA Times, front to back, since 1939."

"Democrat or Republican?"

"He liked Ike but not Nixon. Really liked Bobby Kennedy. He's a small 'l' liberal so far as I can tell."

"How would he do in a race for office?"

"First off, I don't think anything could ever get him to run. . ."

"Any skeletons in the closet?"

"No."

"Where does your father live?"

"West Hollywood."

"Is that the only property he owns?"

"Actually, the family has a small place in El Monte where my father infrequently stays when he works late. A lot of the business records are piled up there."

"You know it's warm in here. How 'bout a stroll over to the elevators and a ride up to the 360 degree, rotating bar on top of the hotel. We can get a *good* drink up there, sightsee a little, and talk some more."

Angela let out a shallow laugh. "Guillermo, I'm married. My husband is right over there." In reality, she was still not married, but a full explanation of her relationship with Robby would only have fueled Guillermo's interest in her. She pointed to Robby and he waved back at her.

"Oh, I'm sorry. I had no idea," Guillermo said. Giving her what he considered his best look, he then said, "Now, how 'bout that drink?" She did not know how to take him at this point. She looked at him for a moment trying to figure him out. She concluded that he still wanted that drink and he was ready to react to whatever reaction she had. If she threw up her hands or called Robby over, Guillermo would say it was just a joke. If she went with him for the drink he would pull out his room key.

Without leaving an opening, she said, as she stepped away, "It's been a pleasure meeting you."

—⊰⊱—

Guillermo called Justice Now on Monday morning and asked for Angela.

"I would like to meet with you and your father to discuss a possible candidacy for him."

"You're kidding."

"No. I'm completely serious."

"Look, Guillermo," she whispered into the phone, "if this is some wild plan to bed me down you are wasting your time."

"It's not. I've given up on that, although it would have been momentous and earth-shaking, I'm sure, at least for you," he paused but she kept mum, "your father is the kind of person we are looking for. Do you know that the Latino vote can control California politics well into the next century?"

"I was never convinced that Latinos voted."

"You're right. How did you know that?"

"I've done voter registration and get-out-the-vote since 1960 — on and off."

"Really?"

"Yes."

"You could be a great asset to your father and to us."

"Who exactly is 'us'?"

"We're a loosely formed organization that identifies a potential race where a Latino candidate has a good chance to succeed."

"Do you have a name?"

"Poder Político (Political Power)."

"Sounds subversive."

"Thank you."

"Look. I'll talk to my dad, see if he'll meet with you, OK?"

"You are an angel, Angela," he said in a sexy whisper.

For her breathy response she chose the following: "And you are the very first man ever to say that to me."

"Really?" he said hopefully.

"No!" she screamed into the receiver, banging the phone down hard and laughing.

They met at the dealership in El Monte. Leo had met smooth talkers before. He did not like Guillermo from the start. The expensive suit. The glasses with tiny lenses. The gold chain dangling from his wrist. The watch. The ring. The cuff-links. The way he smelled.

Mexican mafia, Leo thought. *Is there any way this guy does not either sell or use drugs?*

But what a turnaround after a short while. Guillermo told Leo and Angela how he'd picked crops as a kid with migrant parents, watched them both die of lung disorders. Just like other workers, from DDT, Malathion, you name it. He caught a break and made it to high school in the East Bay. A counselor worked with him and subsidized a study seminar for him for the SAT, the college board test. He had made "A-s" all along in school and over 1400, out of a possible 1600, on the SAT. Harvard was actively seeking minority applicants and he got chosen. Now he wanted to take the next step. His clothes were a mask. Not really him. But it seemed to impress the people he had to impress.

With Guillermo's personal history out of the way, Leo and Angela listened to what he had to say:

They were sitting in a congressional district that had returned a right wing Republican to the US House of Representatives for the last eight years. He called himself a war hero, but somehow, his military records were lost. Nearly two-thirds of the district residents were Latino and only about 5% voted. The election was 14 months away. Minimum cost to run a competent campaign would be $350,000. If they could raise $500,000 to $700,000 they would stand a chance. Republicans, if they realized a fight on their hands, could put up $1,000,000 to $2,000,000 to beat back any Democrat's charge.

"You know, Guillermo," Leo said, "first time I ever voted was for Jimmy Carter as an independent. I think they'll attack me for someone who came late to the party and never really voted before." "Not a problem. We'll turn it to our advantage. We'll use it to encourage other Latino voters. You felt disenfranchised but you saw the light. And here you are, trying to make a difference, and if they register, they can make a difference too."

"Seriously, Guillermo. I'm 58 years old, looking toward retirement. I'm an old dog. I don't know if I can learn all these new tricks, or if I want to."

"It's a chance to do something for your people."

"You know, I graduated from high school to do something for my people, but I really never did anything else after that. I don't think you have the right man."

"What do you think, Angela?" Guillermo asked, turning to her.

"My dad can do whatever he puts his mind to. I'd like to see him run. I don't think I'd like to see him gone from LA. But I would like to see Latino representation in DC."

"Think about it Mr. Figueroa. I'm going to call you, if you don't mind, next week."

"All right."

⸺⸺◉⸺⸺

"Do it."

"Are you sure?" Leo pleaded with Rosa.

"Yes. Do it. You never looked for stardom, Leo. It just keeps finding you. I think it is time for all of these changes. I don't know if these things will happen sooner or later but what's wrong with stepping up and saying I'm a Mexican-American and I'm running for office. Do it."

⸺⸺◉⸺⸺

They met at Justice Now for the first strategy session. There was a conference room and a long table. Angela had suggested the meeting place. She wanted Robby in on it. Guillermo talked about financing, publicity, walking the entire precinct, speeches, events, organizers, endorsements, a campaign office, manning the phones, a pro-candidate theme, an attack theme, and maybe a debate.

Leo did not want to launch any personal attacks but was comfortable with attacking the issues.

"Leo, you will need a campaign manager. I think Angela would be perfect," Guillermo said.

Angela slid back in her seat and shook her head *No.*

"I want Robby to do it," Leo said flatly.

Nothing could have surprised Robby or Angela more.

"Thanks, Leo, but I wouldn't know the first thing."

"Guillermo, you can tell Robby what needs to be done. He'll figure it out."

"Leo, I'm up to my neck in cases around here. I couldn't just drop them. And Angela and I could not afford another hit to our income." "Guillermo," Leo asked, "how much does a campaign manager get? Does he get paid?"

"It depends. Something like this he'd most likely get a salary. Not many would do it for free. Maybe from now 'til then, say $30 to $50,000."

"And where does the money come from?"

"Contributions, fund-raisers, wherever we can source it."

"Aren't there campaign funding laws?"

"Sure. We'll need to account for it. But it is a legitimate expense."

"Well, Robby?" Leo looked at him.

For Robby it was a great opportunity. Personally, he could not say *No.* But first he looked to Angela. From her expression it was clear that she was behind him all the way.

"Sure," Robby said, rising along with Leo for an instant, for a hearty handshake.

"Speaking of contributions, you can invest in yourself."

"I might have a little saved," Leo said.

"Do you know anyone who is real wealthy who would support you?"

"Maybe."

"Well, you can't waste any time where the money is concerned. I'll get you the forms and we'll file the necessary papers. I'll get the media going. Robby, you and I should strategize with what to do with the media. Eventually, Robby, you'll be handling all of it."

⬥

Time flew by. Leo was on the stump putting in long hours. He took a vacation and left the dealerships in the hands of one of Ara's grandsons, Grigor, with whom Leo still found time to check in, on a regular basis. Grigor was sharp as a tack. Before Leo handed things to Grigor completely, he had a meeting with Ara, Hovanes and Antonio in Ara's home library, to tell them the news.

"I may be getting out of the business in about a year and a half." "Retiring?" Ara asked, which is what the trio had concluded after Leo asked them for the meeting.

"Not exactly. They want me to run for Congress?"

"No."

"Yes."

"How did this come up?"

"Angela met a political organizer at some banquet and he came by and talked to me. Next thing I know, I've been recruited."

"Which district?"

"Calloway's."

"But he's Republican. Is he retiring?"

"No. I'm running against him."

"Have you considered your chances?"

"Yes. They couldn't be slimmer."

"So you'll be running as a Democrat?"

"Yes."

"You know," Ara said, "Hovanes and I are Republicans." He looked at Hovanes whose expression never changed. "We contribute a lot to the party."

"I know. I've seen the pictures right over there." Leo pointed to a credenza in the corner with pictures on it, including Ara with many notable Republicans, and others, who Leo did not recognize.

"You know, Leo, we could talk to people. How would you like to run on the Republican side?"

"Gee, Ara, I never liked anybody since Ike, except the Kennedys. I'm not saying I liked Johnson, either, only his domestic policies. And Carter, well, he seems to be stalled, can't really connect with Congress, but, at heart, I'm a Democrat."

"Nothing wrong with Roosevelt I used to say," Ara said, adding, "I voted for him a few times. I'm not trying to talk you into anything, Leo. I guess Grigor can run the car business. What do you think?"

"He's been doing a great job. He's smart. More important. Honest. It might take him a little while to clue in on some of the characters we hire from time to time."

"OK. Guys," Ara said, turning to Hovanes and Antonio, "Grigor OK for you?"

"Yes."

"You coming for campaign money, Leo?" Ara asked.

"No. No I wouldn't think of it."

"You insulting me, Leo. How much you wanting?"

"No. I couldn't ask."

"First rule politics. You asking. Second rule. You taking. Third rule. You forgetting what you did with it. How much you needing to win?"

"Forget it. They say, like $350,000 or more."

"You right, Leo. I think I forgetting it." Ara laughed out loud at himself. "You and Hovanes go taking a little trip to bank. I think it still open. OK?"

"Well, OK. Thanks."

"And you going out there and winning, OK?"

"I'll try my best."

⸺⫷◉⫸⸺

Leo drove Hovanes to the bank. "How is everything, Hovanes?"

"Very good."

"I'm glad to hear it. Your wife, she's OK, and kids, grandkids?"

"They all doing fine."

"Good."

"You wife and kids?" Hovanes asked. "Doing very well."

"I always liking you wife and kids. You wife a beautiful lady. Handsome boy. Elena very sweet. And that Angela. You know my grandson Aram always in love with Angela?"

"No. I didn't know that."

"Oh, yeah. She a little older than him I think, but he always having his eye on her."

"It's a shame he didn't make it back."

Hovanes slowly nodded.

⸺⫷◉⫸⸺

Hovanes made two withdrawals. One from the business reserve account. One from his savings. He got two cashier's checks and put them in an envelope. The bank manager fawned all over him the whole time while Leo waited for him in a chair near the front door. "Here," Hovanes said, handing Leo the envelope, "don't open 'til Christmas." Hovanes had a rare smile and a little twinkle in his eye.

"No. You opening with campaign manager or you wife, OK?"

"Sure. And thanks."

⁓⊙⁓

Leo asked Angela and Robby for dinner. Rosa made everyone's favorite, enchiladas *estilo mole poblano* (in spicy chocolate sauce). She also made *flan* (custard) for dessert.

"What's the occasion?" Angela asked.

"We have our first contribution. It's from Avakian Enterprises," Leo announced.

"I thought they were Republicans," Angela spouted.

"They are. But they're helping us out."

"Very nice of them. How much?"

"I don't know. We can open the envelope now or after dinner."

Rosa spoke, "Why not open it now?"

"OK. Here goes. Oops. There's two checks in here." Leo gathered them up and held them close to his chest. The look on his face said it all.

"How big are they?"

"One is $350,000 from the business. The other is $500,000 from Hovanes' personal account."

"I always thought he was a closet Democrat," Angela said, smiling uncontrollably, along with everyone else at the table. Robby jumped up, started a hand clasp and led everyone through the house singing *Hava Nagila*.

⁓⊙⁓

Nothing went smoothly. Getting out the vote proved as difficult as it had ever been. Yet despite a dismally slow start, Leo began to climb in the polls. Voter registration remained key, and unfortunately, lagged behind name recognition. Robby built an infrastructure — mainly student volunteers — college age — to canvas neighborhoods. It started to work. Pedro and Joe D'Amico got involved. Pedro organized the volunteers. Joe created a computer base and a program to monitor all aspects of the campaign. He even concocted a variety of tracking polls.

The Republicans paid little mind to Leo. The district had been sewn up for years. But when Republican polling showed a 20% name recognition for Leo and even higher recognition as a candidate who had won the Congressional Medal Honor they started to flood the district with literature focusing on Calloway's war record. This confused many.

To a casual observer it seemed that Calloway had won the medal. The Republicans were also working on a TV ad to show a combat sequence, a medal ceremony from a distance, and Calloway smiling and saluting, with the American Flag billowing behind him.

Robby countered with TV ads in a big way — candidate and family — candidate's message to a crowd of voters — and candidate war hero. Robby went for TV ads on Channels 5, 9, 11, 13 and 34 (the Spanish language channel) during the game show, and sitcom re-run hour, which was just after the nightly news hour. He ran the ads every night for two weeks straight. As a result, Leo's recognition jumped to 42%.

But Robby could not match the rise in recognition with the rise in voter registration, still hovering in very low numbers for Latinos. He redoubled his efforts to close the gap.

Financing was not a problem. In fact contributions started coming in from movie people once they found out it was Rosa's husband who was running for Congress. Rosa had no idea how many friends she had made over the years and how many were willing to throw their support behind her.

Robby asked for a debate. When the other side refused, Robby got the press involved to investigate the refusal.

"There had not been a refusal. When time permitted the debate would take place at the local VFW Hall," said Bradford Sutton, Calloway's campaign manager. The VFW Hall was a place where Calloway was blindly viewed as a war hero.

Robby wanted a televised debate. The local PBS Station was interested. The debate over the debate between Robby and Sutton lasted throughout the summer. Neither candidate had any opposition in the Primary Election so the debate, if it ever took place, would be head to head. Time kept running down and the debate window was closing.

Robby got a call from Sutton, but not about the debate issue.

"I need to talk to you, in private. Something's come up with your candidate. I need to run it by you. I don't want to give it to the Press."

"What is it?"

"Not over the phone. I think it's best if only the two of us discuss it. It's major."

"How so?"

"I can't say. Please for your own good and that of your candidate."

"OK. When and where?"

"Tomorrow. Clifton's Cafeteria on Broadway, about 11 a.m. OK?"

"You know," Robby said, "I've seen the 'Godfather' too many times to buy into this. How 'bout I plant myself somewhere, call you and have you meet me there?"

"Suit yourself. This is for real."

"OK."

"One more thing, Robby. To quench your own paranoia you better make it a place without old style toilets with a chain flush."

"Very funny."

Leo sat across from Robby at Robby's desk in the campaign office. It was late.

"I have no idea what it could be, Leo. Do you have any idea?" Leo shook his head *No*.

"Leo, you have to tell me if there is anything. Anyone in your past? You owe gambling money? You killed someone? You have a mistress. They thrive on this stuff."

"No, Robby. Nothing I can think of."

"What about the Avakians? Antonio?"

"I don't know. The Avakians can be colorful. But I see them as hardworking and honest. Antonio is straight-laced."

"Rosa?"

"Oh. Maybe this is about her. She's illegal."

"Damn."

"What can we do?"

"I'll start the process to get her citizenship. How has she worked here for so long?"

"She has a social security number. Fake."

"OK. We'll deal with it. Like Guillermo Augustin says, 'We'll turn it to our advantage.'"

———⸺《○》⸺———

Robby had Bradford Sutton meet him at Justice Now. They had the conference room to themselves.

"Robby, this is not easy for me. I like Leo. I wish he was on our side. I wish you were on our side. I wish he were running in another race. Not this one. But I've got Calloway and he's a tiger."

"A tiger, a tiger? Did Calloway really see combat in Vietnam?"

"I'm not going to go there with you, Robby."

"Come on, Brad."

"Robby, you're the only person, I'm sure of, who saw combat in Vietnam."

"How'd you know that?"

"Let me lay it all out. I know it's going to hit you far too close to home. I might have found some things out that the candidate himself doesn't even know. About people very close to him. I want you to know something first. I went to night school just like you. I'm a lawyer too. Fortunately, Calloway is not a client of mine. I'm just wearing one hat here. Campaign manager. They handed me all the authority. They expect me to use it. They aren't going to second guess me. But I'm at risk here too. Depending on how this goes down my days in politics could be numbered. They want blood-and-guts campaign managers. They shun the lessons of Watergate. They don't give a shit about them. It's politics as usual for them."

Robby listened.

"I'm going to say what I have to say and I'm telling you that you will be the fourth person to know this. My two operatives. Me. And you. My two operatives answer to me alone and can be trusted." Sutton took out some notes. "So here goes," he said, sometimes gazing at his notes, other times not:

"My operatives have ways of interviewing people without misleading them but still getting a surprising amount of information. Most ordinary people will talk to them and tell them what they know.

Even law enforcement will share things with them. It's uncanny." He paused. "Carmen Fernandez, you know who she is, don't you?"

"Yes."

"And Rosa Figueroa were prostitutes in Tijuana before they illegally entered the United States in 1937."

Robby kept the same stern look on his face that he had brought into the meeting. In reality, the news about his mother-in-law was such a shock, his facial expression did not have time to catch up to it.

"What proof do you have?"

"Well, a girl, Carmen had dumped years ago, named Ann Sampson, a lesbian lover of Carmen, revealed that Carmen told her that she and Rosa had spent a year in a night club on Revolucion Avenue in Tijuana dancing nude and turning tricks. They saved their money and were smuggled across the border, ending up in LA. You can check this out with your mother-in-law," he said. But seeing Robby glaring at him, he meekly added, "or Carmen."

Robby kept staring at him.

"I don't know if the candidate is aware of his wife's past."

"Is that it?"

"No."

"What else do you have?"

"The candidate's father shot and killed a prominent doctor, named Monson, in Utah."

"And...?"

"The local Sheriff covered for the candidate's father. But forensics shows and a few loose-lipped neighbors say the doctor threatened the candidate's high school buddy, Eduardo Velasco, with a rifle after Velasco crippled the doctor's son. The doctor took a shot at Velasco and the candidate's father blew the doctor's brains out. The doctor's son wouldn't talk to my operatives about anything. Anyway, the candidate's father shot the doctor in cold blood."

"What about self-defense?"

"The doctor never saw the candidate's father or the gun he was holding and the candidate's father was not defending himself."

"What about defending the candidate's buddy, or trying to stop a crime?"

"Not at this point since now the prosecutor can add obstruction of justice, which is, itself a crime. The local prosecutor would likely want to parade the candidate's father before a grand jury, who are all white, to get to the bottom of it. The jury might indict. Then there's jail time for the dad, or bail. A trial. The candidate's dad is too old. He'd never make it. The Sheriff, who would only get in the way at this point, is in the hospital, dying of lung cancer as we speak."

"Anything else?"

"I suppose you realize your wife was conceived out of wedlock and you and her are not legally married."

Not a stone unturned, Robby thought. "What's the deal?" Robby asked.

"The candidate cites personal reasons and drops out of the race. Real simple. None of what I dug up goes anywhere."

Robby continued his fixed gaze on Sutton.

"I want to make sure I have this correct. You are an attorney. You value our collegiality. You are saving me, my candidate, and his family from incalculable trauma were this information to become public. You have taken precautions in that regard and have not shared the information with your candidate, who you and I both know, would leak it to the press in a heartbeat."

"That's right," Sutton said smiling, thinking he had Robby on his side.

"So you think blackmailing me with this information falls within the four corners of a lawyer's code of ethics? You think this information has any impact on the ability of the candidate as a future lawmaker? You think this information has relevance in this campaign?"

"No. I don't. But your campaign is doomed if it comes out. And you know it. I did not come here to fight or debate. I did not have to come here at all. This is politics, and it is all I can give you. Take it or leave it."

"I'll call you soon." They stood up. Sutton automatically offered his hand. Robby's adrenaline accounted for the bone crushing grasp that ensued.

⸺◉⸺

Robby went straight to Leo. "Leo, they did some private investigating on you and your whole family."

"Can they do that?"

"Yes."

"I mean, is it legal?"

"It depends, but that doesn't really matter at this point."

"Well, what do they say?"

"There's some innocuous stuff about me and Angela not being married, that Angela was conceived out-of-wedlock. . ."

"Geez. Would they really bring up things like that or are they just trying to get to you?"

"I don't know how far they would go."

"Well, anything else?"

"Two things. Both major. One has to do with your father, the other with Rosa." Robby paused, trying to formulate the right words.

"Tell me, Robby."

"Your dad, apparently shot and killed a Dr. Monson."

"No. That was the Sheriff."

"I'm afraid not. The Sheriff did a complete cover-up for your dad."

"How is that possible?"

"I don't know. We need to talk to your dad about it. He could be indicted, arrested, tried, sent to jail. There is no statute of limitations for murder."

"Let's call Eddy," Leo said.

Robby walked over to the door of his office and opened it to see who was around. He closed and locked the door. Leo gave him the number. He dialed it and put the call on speaker phone.

"Hello?" A woman answered.

"Is Eddy in?" Robby asked.

"He's just outside. I'll get him."

After nearly half a minute, "Hello."

"Eddy?" Leo spoke up.

"Leo?"

"Yeah. I'm here with Robby. We're on a speaker phone. We're working on my campaign."

"How's it going?"

"Not bad. But I need to find out something from you about Dr. Monson?"

"Which one?"

"The old one."

"Sure."

"How did he die?"

"What do you know, Leo?"

"I'm being told that the Sheriff did not actually kill him, like everybody, including you and my dad, always said."

"What's the difference?"

"The difference is if I don't play ball here they'll be carting my dad off to the big house."

"We would have told you, Leo, and we should have, maybe, but we felt it was best, the less people who knew the better."

"So what happened?"

"I broke Avery's hands. You know he's all crippled?"

"Yeah. I thought a jack collapsed on his hands or something like that."

"Well, that's what he said after I told him that I'd kill him if he told the truth about what happened to his hands."

"Were you drunk?"

"No. I always wanted him to pay for Beatriz. I finally confronted him, lost it, and broke all of his fingers."

"So then what happened?"

"Apparently, a couple years down the line, young Monson told old Monson I did it and old Monson came after me with a rifle. He blew my arm open and your dad let him have it with one of his .45s. The Sheriff showed up and had a talk with your dad. And took his gun. He told your dad not to talk to anyone, ever, about what happened and as far as your dad was supposed to know, the Sheriff shot Monson when he wouldn't surrender his weapon."

"But you were an eyewitness."

"Yeah. The Sheriff had the same talk with me."

"Did anyone else see this happen?"

"Two or three people, maybe. The Sheriff made a report and included himself, me and old Monson as the only witnesses. No statements were taken."

Leo turned to Robby. "What do you think?"

"We'll have to discuss this once we get off the phone," Robby said.

"I'm sorry Leo," Eddy said, "but imagine what it would have been like for your dad in front of a jury here. I think the Sheriff did the right thing."

"It's OK, Eddy. I do too. Say, I heard the Sheriff is hospitalized, dying of cancer. Do you know how he is?"

"I saw him a couple days ago. His hair's gone. Couldn't weigh more than a hundred pounds. Poor guy messed his bed while I was there. He's on oxygen. You know he was a heavy smoker."

"Yeah."

"Anyway, they have him sedated. He sleeps most of the time. Tries to cough, to bring something up. He's a ghost of himself. When he talks to you, it's just a whisper, he's the same person on the inside but unrecognizable on the outside. Same good man, though. He doesn't have much time. He asked me to give you his best."

"If you see him, tell him I send my best. And if he needs anything, let me know, will you?"

"Sure. So how should I deal with this? You're not going to talk to your father, are you?"

"No. I won't. I'll deal with it on this end. You keep on like you have been. Treat it the same. Hopefully this whole thing will blow over."

"OK, Leo. Good luck."

"Thanks, Eddy."

"You're welcome."

They hung up.

"What do you think, Robby?"

"If you drop out of the race, none of this will see the light of day."

"Is there any other way to get them not to use this?"

"I don't think so."

"Do we have anything on them?"

"No. Not really."

"Have we done this kind of investigation on them?"

"No."

"Should we have done it?"

"I don't know. It's something I've heard about, maybe if I had been more experienced, I'd have done it, and I'd have answers for you now. But I didn't want to roll in the mud with the other side."

"But now we're up to our hips in mud, aren't we."

"Yes we are."

"Well, what is the rest of it about Rosa?" Robby paused.

Leo said, "It's about her being illegal, right?"

Robby paused another instant, "Look Leo, we don't have to go into that if you decide not to run because of your father."

"I guess I'll have to withdraw but I want to discuss this with Rosa and Angela first."

"Sure."

"OK. When."

"Tonight. It can't wait. Come for dinner."

"OK."

Everyone agonized over the predicament. Rosa had asked Pedro and Joe to come over too. Leo and Robby agreed to focus on the issue regarding Leo's father only. Neither one of them brought Rosa into the picture as an obstacle. And only Robby had the full story about Rosa and Carmen, since he was able to sidestep and put off Rosa's issues with Leo.

"Isn't it really blackmail?" Rosa asked Robby.

"In a way, yes."

"What if you go back to Sutton and tell him you are going to expose his tactics?"

"It's not that simple."

"If the information gets out, the DA in Utah will be forced to indict. I don't see it any other way. The Sheriff could also be indicted. Eddy, too. If they can't get Don Pedro on murder, they can get him, and everyone else, on obstruction of justice. It's a no-win situation. It is not something we want to see happen."

"So that's it. Leo's campaign is dead in its tracks?"

"I think so."

"Do you think if you told Sutton that you taped him," Rosa asked, "and you are going to turn it over to authorities that he would back down?"

"We don't have a tape."

"Just if he thought you would turn him in, though?"

"It's not a good bluff. Without a tape, I wouldn't try it."

"But if you had a tape, would he back down?"

"He might."

"Can't you tell him you taped him?"

"I could but … but he'll want the tape. He'll want to listen to it and destroy it."

Joe D'Amico spoke up. "Could you have taped him?"

"What do you mean?"

"Was the opportunity there to have taped him?"

"Yes. I could have."

"Would there have been ambient sounds?"

"Ambient sounds?"

"Besides you and him talking, were there other sounds?"

"Not really. We were in my conference room at Justice Now."

"Where could you have hidden the recorder?"

"Under the table, in some plants, in a briefcase, maybe."

"Can you remember the conversation?"

"Not word for word."

"How much of it could you write down?"

"80, 90 per cent, maybe."

"Here's what we can do. You write down everything you can remember. We'll go to Justice Now and test a recorder. You can play you on the recording and we'll have to get someone to play Sutton."

"He'll know it's not him."

"Everyone sounds different on tape than he does to himself. We'll see. But is this even worth trying?"

"I think Sutton would do anything to save his own skin, so I think, if he believed that the tape were real, he would back off. After all, unfortunately, Calloway still leads in the poll of likely voters. Sutton may be convinced that he does not need to pull out all the stops to win."

Rosa looked at her husband,

"What do you say, Leo?"

"Let's give it a try. Even if Sutton figures it out he'll likely admire Robby for turning into someone as sleazy as himself. And so what if Sutton figures it out — that it's not him on the tape — I'll drop out." Turning to Robby, Leo said, "Robby, once you have the script ready I want to read it."

Robby never looked more under pressure.

⟪◉⟫

At the campaign office Leo read Robby's account of his meeting with Bradford Sutton, then turned to Robby.

"Rosa never finds out about this."

"I know, Leo. Do you still want to run?"

"I think this Sutton character will crack if we do this right. We're going to have to have someone play Sutton on tape. You know him. Is there anyone who would sound like him?"

"Actually there is someone in my office who sounds a lot like him. I think he'd do it. And he'd keep all of this in strict confidence. He wouldn't want to end up in jail with the rest of us."

"I guess we can count on Joe D'Amico to keep it in strict confidence, too?"

"Of course."

"Even keep it from Pedro."

"For sure. I'll talk to Joe. Don't worry."

"OK."

After some experimentation the plot was executed. It took hours to get what Robby believed was a tape sufficiently realistic to convince Sutton he was actually on it.

Robby called Bradford Sutton. "We need to meet," Robby said.

"OK."

"This evening. Eight o'clock. Same place?"

"Sure."

There were only a couple lights on at Justice Now. It was ghostly quiet.

"Bradford, I've spoken with the candidate and he is not the kind of person who can be threatened or blackmailed."

"Would he let his whole family go down the tubes?"

"No."

"So?"

"He said he is willing to take you down with him."

"Me? What do you mean by that?"

"Bradford, I've got you on tape."

"What?"

"Our last conversation here. I've got you on tape."

"You taped me?"

"Yes."

"That's illegal."

"No. I can tape you. I just can't use it without your consent."

"And you'll never get it."

"Unless you leave the information you have on my candidate's family buried, I *will* use it and *your career will be over.*"

"You're out of your mind."

"Maybe."

"What are you proposing?"

"What you have on Leo never sees the light of day and I will destroy the tape. Besides Calloway is so far ahead in the polls, is any of this really necessary?"

"Where's the tape?"

"Right here."

"Can I listen to it?"

"Sure."

Robby slipped the cartridge into an old tape recorder. It ran silently for a while, then there was some shuffling about and a door opening and closing. The sounds were not altogether clear. Rather muffled.

Bradford Sutton listened, thinking he never sounded like himself on tape. He generally remembered the content of the conversation. Given his heightened sense of excitement at that moment, the fact the conversation was not verbatim never entered his thinking. Robby's voice was several times louder than Sutton's from the tape, and clearer. There were muted gaps, where Robby could not remember what had been said, left off the tape.

"Where did you have the recorder?" "In a briefcase on my side of the table."

"Well, I don't think much of the quality. I'm not sure anyone would really understand it," Sutton argued.

"I'm told we can hire someone to pull up all the words and transcribe them into booklet form. I would do that anyway to send copies to all the news agencies."

"You could end up in jail over this, you know."

"Well this whole thing is a hell of a crap shoot for both of us, now isn't it?"

"I'll tell you what. Let's make a deal."

'"What do you have in mind, Bradford?"

"You keep your tape and I keep my information. Both under wraps. When the election is over, we'll have a drink and a mini-bonfire."

"Do you mean it?"

"I do."

"Then done."

"Good."

"And Bradford, I'll even throw in a copy of the tape from this meeting."

"You scoundrel!"

Robby was reminded of an anecdote from college. "Did you ever here the story about Andrew Jackson when it comes to scoundrels?"

"No."

"On a footpath on Pennsylvania Avenue strode Andy Jackson in one direction and his arch-rival, Henry Clay, in the other. It was a very narrow path. When they came together Jackson stood his ground and said, 'I never step aside for scoundrels.' Bowing from the waist and stepping aside, Clay graciously extended his arm with a flair, and beckoning Jackson to pass, said, 'I always do.'"

"But you think I'm the only scoundrel here, don't you Robby?"

"Not really."

⎯⎯•(O)•⎯⎯

Robby told Leo about the deal. In the months ahead Leo closed the gap in the polls. In the debate, Calloway showed himself both skillful and knowledgeable. Real smooth in fact. Maybe too smooth. Leo, down to earth by comparison, held his own. Leo, drawing from stories he had followed in the LA Times, came up time and again with details effectively correcting Calloway's accounts of certain events, and made some rather humorous comments, keeping the studio audience and questioners in his corner all night.

In the end each side spun the debate declaring a victory for itself. In the last two weeks of the campaign Leo shot ahead of Calloway in an LA Times straw poll.

But Joe D'Amico was concerned. His computer, no matter which way he drew on the data in it, kept spitting out a squeaker to Calloway.

The day after the election Robby sat down with Bradford Sutton in the bar at *Le Chambord* restaurant on Wilshire Boulevard in Beverly Hills. Robby recognized Robert Morley, the English actor from "African Queen" sitting with others in a corner booth.

There was no bonfire for Robby and Sutton. But the promised exchange took place.

Robby handed Sutton the tape cartridges and got in return the *dossier* on Leo and his family. Each assured the other that there were no more copies of any of the material.

"Congratulations," Robby said.

"You put up a great fight, Robby, but you never had a chance."

"When did you know you would win, Brad?"

"From the start. I did not believe there was any way to mobilize the Latino vote. You got the highest percentage ever to the polls in any race anywhere but you still couldn't win. You had the numbers on your side but not enough registered voters. Your day will come. But not for a long time."

"We tried."

"Yeah. Tell me, will Leo run again?"

"I don't know."

"I know this is prying, but I've always been curious, how did he take the news about his wife?"

"I don't know. He never said a word to me."

"Well, congratulate him on his effort. I wish he were Republican."

"He liked Ike, you know."

"But not Tricky Dick?"

"No."

"Good luck, Robby. See you down the road." They shook hands.

Leo met with Hovanes and Ara. He told them he'd hand over what was left after a final accounting and asked them if they wanted him to repay them.

"Look, Leo," Ara said, "you doing what you have to with campaigning money. And you coming seeing us next time you running. We never turning our back on you. You a good man."

Hovanes, nodding in accord, looked like liquid blur to Leo, whose heart was warming and whose eyes were beginning to well up.

The next summer Leo and Rosa commandeered a demo Vanagon, camper model, from Grigor at the El Monte dealership and took a road trip to Yellowstone National Park, stopping at the family farm in Utah along the way to fill the empty seats with nieces and nephews.

When they returned to the farm from Yellowstone, Don Pedro was not doing very well. Leo and Rosa decided to stay in Utah for a while and help out where they could.

The doctor put Pedro in the hospital for a week to rest him for walking pneumonia. Pedro was still weak when he came out. He'd be 80 soon. It was tough to get Don Pedro to rest. He had a lot of well-wishers and he did not want to turn anyone away.

One morning, Don Pedro had Leo and Eddy haul his bed into the living room so he could keep up with the comings and goings of family and friends. He left everything, from under the bed, exactly where it lay. On one of his out-of-beds to use the bathroom he rummaged through the things on the bedroom floor and picked up an old machete. He brought it into the living room and set it under the bed.

After dinner that evening, Don Pedro asked Rosa to read to him. "My eyes are not so good," he said.

"Sure, Don Pedro. What would you like me to read?"

"You know, I have this old book.'The Adventures of Huckleberry Finn.' Come sit next to me and read it to me, would you?"

"Sure."

Rosa climbed onto the bed and made herself comfortable. She used to read to her children this way. Leo pulled up a chair close to the bed.

"Rosa, you don't mind if I lean against you and try to follow the words, do you?" Pedro asked.

"Not at all."